COME TO THE EDGE

A young woman tells the story of her decision to take a break from suburban life by moving to a shambolic, draughty farmhouse in a scenic country valley. Along with the farmhouse comes a new companion, a widowed survivalist called Cassandra White. Her crazy, utopian dream is to stop rich city-dwellers buying up rural second homes. Others who become involved include a banker — and scores of poor and elderly people with nowhere to go . . .

JOANNA KAVENNA

COME TO
THE EDGE

Complete and Unabridged

ULVERSCROFT
Leicester

First published in Great Britain in 2012 by
Quercus
London

First Large Print Edition
published 2013
by arrangement with
Quercus
London

The moral right of the author has been asserted

A catalogue record for this book is available
from the British Library.

ISBN 978–1–4448–1571–9

Published by
F. A. Thorpe (Publishing)
Anstey, Leicestershire

Set by Words & Graphics Ltd.
Anstey, Leicestershire
Printed and bound in Great Britain by
T. J. International Ltd., Padstow, Cornwall

This book is printed on acid-free paper

To the real Cassandra White

Come to the edge, he said.
They said, We are afraid.
Come to the edge, he said.
They came. He pushed them.
They flew.

Written in the spirit of Guillaume
Apollinaire by Christopher Logue

1

One moment Cassandra White was telling me I was a useless fool and that I couldn't milk a goat to save my life; the next she was firing shots in the air and saying we had to burn down Beckfoot Cottage.

It's strange how events got out of hand. Certainly Cassandra got out of hand, and that morning we were running up the hill away from the farm, and the wind was wailing and the birds were screeching in the hedges.

The whole place was trembling in the storm, and Cassandra was saying, 'Don't panic, I'm going to fucking blast them to smithereens if they come anywhere near us,' and waving a gun in the air, as if that would help anyone.

'I think you should throw that in the bushes,' I was saying because I was always more of a coward than her.

'Don't be ridiculous, how will I get rid of the bastards without a gun?' she replied, and I suppose I did wonder then how it came to this, how a nice girl from the suburbs like me who never bothered anyone in her life ended up scrambling up a hillside in a howling gale with a gun-toting maniac.

'But they'll shoot at us.'

'So what?'

'Well, so we might die.' We were shouting at each other because the wind was so high-pitched and raving, and all the trees were bending around us.

'Death is not important. You have to think of the bigger picture,' she said. 'Have you still not learned anything at all?'

Really that was unfair, I'd learned a lot. I'd learned how to milk a goat, and how to deal with the physical and spiritual implications of a thunderbox, and how to cultivate a line of marrows. I'd learned that all things being equal then it was best to do whatever Cassandra told me.

Except now I was beginning to wonder if that was really the right policy decision after all and if it wasn't time to reassess the situation.

We were halfway up the hill now, passing the yew trees, and then we vaulted over a stile and I could hear the sheep rustling in the bracken as I landed. The stream was gushing down the hillside. Then Cassandra turned and said — in a tone of childish glee, as if it was Christmas and she had just seen her teetering stack of presents — 'Just look at the valley!' and I turned and saw the valley was burning.

The houses were on fire.

Flames rising, and billowing clouds of smoke merging with the storm sky above.

The mountains obscured by smoke and cloud.

Like beacons, the burning houses were like beacons in the valley below.

'Good, they've set up a roadblock over by the turning to Birker Fell,' said Cassandra — pointing down at a line of lights and the distant sound of horns. Police lights flashing in the misty valley, and sometimes a quick burst of a siren, as if to tell everyone to calm down and stop setting things on fire. It didn't look as if that tactic was really working for them.

Cassandra was staring down at the scene with her eyes reflecting the engulfing pyres beneath. She had her gun clasped tightly to her bosom, nursing it to her, and I thought it was ironic that her husband got blown to pieces in a desert and now she was going to get herself blasted across the fells he called home.

'They're actually doing it,' she said. 'They're finally taking it back.'

'They're not taking it back, they're burning it down,' I said.

'The stone walls will survive. The buildings

3

will endure, the integral buildings. It'll just be all the interior crap which will get burned.'

And it was certainly getting burned, burned in a giant bonfire, a fireworks display of pure rage.

From this rock you have a grand view of the valley, from the high arch of mountains to the west and along the winding, snaking riverbed towards the Hardknott and Wrynose passes. Beyond that — Coniston, the Langdale Valley, the real idyllic tourist trail. For a moment I forgot about Cassandra's whole 'The land is ours' thing and perceived the clear fact that if we didn't get killed we were definitely going to jail. For a moment I felt sick and as if I might faint, but then I heard a dense pile of timber crashing to the ground, some luxury extension collapsing under the heat, and that focused my mind a little. I thought of all those fine furnishings blistered and pocked with flame. I thought of what the valley would look like when the fires died down. Scorched earth. And all those shattered husks of buildings. Piles of ash.

Like the aftermath of a war.

'We have to get to Beckfoot,' said Cassandra, and she turned and started running up the path again, a lanky figure, flame-hair flowing behind her, like a fire spirit, and the valley all liquid with fire beneath her.

I was about to follow her, but I stopped to take another look. And I was gazing down at the flames jagged against the ancient rocks and the thick black clouds and I suddenly thought but how had this happened? Whose idea was it to torch everything if the scheme failed? Who stored the canisters of petrol in the houses? Who handed out the matches?

I remembered Cassandra standing in the garden earlier firing three shots in the air, and I wondered who told them that three shots fired from White Farm would mean Armageddon! BURN EVERYTHING!

Above there was the insect whirr of a helicopter, some police outfit coming in to land.

And now I was hesitating; I was there on the rock not knowing where to turn.

2

Until I went to live with Cassandra White I'd never lived in the country before. I lived in the suburbs of a provincial town, and I liked it there. Suburbia was my chosen idyll, and I was a devout worshipper of my personal pile of bricks, bricks my husband and I were paying off one by one, until the glorious day we would own them all. And we were blessed and as well as the gleaming bricks we aspired to own we had our polished cars in their garage shrine and our recently reslabbed stone drive to rumble the wheels on . . .

And our happy humming fridge

And our flat-pack totems

And our garden with one water feature spewing water from a hole in a triangle, the triangle representing the all-encompassing OM or perhaps the sea of time, or the interconnectedness of all things, and another water feature casting a constant trickle of water over a soothing basket of pebbles. That we shall know the name of eternity . . .

Our CDs and DVDs mounted on the wall

The background whirr of electronics

The halogen bulbs in the kitchen ceiling,

each light picking out its own particular spot of mock marble finish

And one day if we were really virtuous and if the Lord poured blessings on our head we hoped we might have . . . oh, how we hoped and how we feared we were not worthy . . . underfloor heating . . . AAAAAA-MEN.

And lo, we had decided to bring a child into this mini-paradise, but the Lord had not so far favoured my womb, and so my life was rich in ovulation sticks and the smell of piss drying on plastic and a calendar with KEY DATES shaded in red and POSSIBLY KEY DATES in green and the rest of the calendar barren and uninteresting, nothing days which I must live through to arrive at my next KEY DATES. And on these rouged-in days I would persuade my husband into mechanical sex, procreative sex, arranging ourselves into the advised positions and twining our limbs together not for pleasure but simply to bang out a child.

Bang bang bang, there was my husband hammering away, trying to forge flesh from my womb and there was the clock ticking above my head, telling me that I was no longer young, better hurry better hurry, and there was my heart pounding in the small hours when I lay awake thinking that I would never have a child.

Ticktocktick, January and the rain falls heavily on the vintage-look windows of our bedroom and wakes me in the small hours.

March and I walk in the garden and sit by the water features and think OM OM OM.

June and I buy a luxury juicer so I will be enriched in fertility.

August and I stand in the bathroom looking at my ovulation sticks lined up for that month, ready to receive the anointing fountain of piss.

October and I turn circles round the garden thinking OM let me conceive OM OM.

December and the year ends and we all begin again . . .

Bang Bang Bang

Ticktocktick . . .

All that was dull and life-stripping enough, but I might have carried on with it for years had my husband not pulled the plug. Surely I would have meandered along, in that twilight suburban half-life, but my husband rudely fired off the emergency flares, tugged on his parachute and pressed EJECT.

★　★　★

He did it all one ordinary inoffensive morning in our house when I was waking to the sound of the *Today* programme, and the light was streaming round the edges of my immaculate white Roman blinds onto the glittering shape of the mirror. And my husband was handing me a cup of coffee, which he never did.

'What's this for?' I said, half-asleep.

'I want to tell you something,' he said. My husband was — still is, no doubt — a chinless man. Handsome in a cherubic way, but certainly lacking a chin. Not that I'm anything wondrous to behold either, but now it was me looking up at my husband — his broad face, full cheeks, the hairs in his nostrils and his furry ears and he said, 'You won't like it.'

It's true I didn't like it, though there was something inevitable about the image he advanced — a tall vivacious girl called Lydie, barely twenty-five and glinting with the hard perfection of youth, glinting her perfect pearly teeth at him, and saying, 'Come hither and come hither' — I only imagine this, never having witnessed it, perhaps I'm traducing the sensual splendour of their union, rendering it in trite phrases and warping everything through the lens of my fury, and it must have been splendid enough because my husband was telling me that he wanted to leave.

'That's a surprise,' I said.

'I don't know what to say,' he said.
'Is she pregnant?'
'No.'

★ ★ ★

He was irreproachable in all things, offering me money and other consolations, the iPod, the Mac, the flat-screen TV, all of them to immure me to lonely despair, he clearly thought, and his virtuous pose only slipped once when he said, tactlessly but admittedly with the facts on his side: 'Also, let's face it, I want a child, and I think you and I know things have stalled on that front.' My husband, a kind man, regretted what he said but said it all the same . . .

OM SHANTI SHANTI SHANTI I shout as I stand in the garden kicking in the water features, with my feet wet and my face wet with self-pitying tears and OM Bastard OM I shout as I smash the consoling basket of pebbles and snap the little valve and the water stops. The water dries up and then ceases forever. And I am left with nothing but the unpalatable truth.

Truth . . . unheralded visitor to our suburban bang-house smashed the doors open and thrust me into the cold light of day, carrying a backpack and a suitcase with my ego all ripped and torn.

Truth thrust me up the M6 and to this wind-lashed house in the middle of nowhere, with the pipes jangling in the night and the smell of mould and decay thick in the air.

Truth and to be more precise an advert I read one day, an advert which stuck in my head until my husband made his great announcement.

Wanted, companion in rural life. Can be male or female preferably not completely young, but not entirely decrepit either. Widow living alone on farm, needs help with sprawling property and various plans for improvement. Ample room for lodging. No stipend but no expenses — food included, bills paid. Idyllic setting, but hard work required. Apply to Cassandra White . . .

So I applied to Cassandra White.

3

You drive while cursing the fates.

I went from the Midlands to the M6, and then I drove in a rage up the motorway, swerving around lorries and sometimes pelted by rainstorms. My car buffeted by winds. And on my lips a refrain, 'The bastard the bastard,' not knowing if I meant my husband or God or Lydie or myself or everyone and any divinity I could summon jumbled in together. I blamed myself and then I blamed everyone else. I was the sole agent of my paltry destiny and then I was merely the hapless victim of circumstances. The evil genius was my husband. Then the evil genius was the God of the Old Testament, or maybe the wanton indifferent universe, moving on its implacable course to wherever it was heading.

Junction 14 for historic Stafford, fortified by Ethelfleda, Lady of Mercia and daughter of Alfred the Great.

Stop at Junction 14 to see Stafford Castle.

A fine Norman construction.

Stop at Junction 14 for a fascinating excursion into early modern history.

Or put your head down and drive . . .

Divorce on the grounds of infertility, I thought. Divorce on the grounds of mutual boredom and creeping revulsion. Divorce on the grounds of acute and grinding malaise. Divorce on the grounds of a potbelly and flabby inner thighs. Divorce on the grounds of being a flawed human, but unloved and thereby grotesque.

Junction 16 for the Railway Age Heritage Centre.

Illustrating Crewe's industrial past.

At Junction 17 I knew I was a fool and should have seen it coming.

At Junction 18 I blamed my husband for being such an all-singing all-dancing ball of scum.

At Junction 19 I wanted to find Lydie and break her bones, and I entertained myself until Junction 20 with a sustained fantasy of her lovely long legs all jumbled and smashed, as I stood over her with a leer of triumph on my face.

At Junction 21 I wanted to get out of my head, so I stopped in a motorway service station jam-packed with the clinically obese, moving their saggy frames in search of burgers and coffee. It was a Grade A convention of the gone to seed. Anthropologically it was rich in exemplars. Here they were, fat parents with their cloned fat children, slurping and munching. The obese on parade. The spectacle makes you reassess the species and its future on the planet. You begin to think it wouldn't be so bad if we all became extinct; the planet could survive without these lumpen concrete service stations and their lumpen waddling inmates. The planet would turn and turn again, and gratefully forget us all.

You have been junked up. You may now leave the building.

I got back on the motorway again. We all got back on the motorway, with the sour smell of vinegar in our mouths, in our hair, grease settling in our bellies. We all drove on. Eyes on the road, the radio saying, 'Beeep beeep beeeeeeeep. The headlines at three o'clock.'

Junction 23 for the Haydock Holiday Inn. The perfect backdrop for your midlife crisis.

★ ★ ★

All I knew about Cassandra White was that she sounded forthright and vaguely eccentric on the phone. She had a house and a couple of acres, she told me. 'I am mostly self-sufficient,' she added, and I thought that must mean chickens and a goat, something

14

small-scale and bucolic. 'Do you like gardening?'

'Oh yes,' I said, though really I never did any. I paid a man called Cyril to do the garden. But I imagined it couldn't be so hard.

'Do you mind living in a cold house, where you have to use a wood-burning stove to cook?'

'No,' I said.

'Do you mind collecting rainwater to wash your clothes?'

'No.'

'Do you mind eating vegetables only when they are in season and never shopping in a supermarket?'

'No.'

It wasn't that I was lying. I simply had no idea if I minded or not, never having been required to do any of these things. Besides I was desperate.

'I would like to experience something different,' I said.

'Well, it'll certainly be different,' she said, and then she made a sound which was more like a cackle than a laugh.

★　★　★

Junction 25 for a northern city, full of monuments to the fallen. Junction 27 for the

15

north — south divide writ large.

At Junction 28 I nearly got out and wept, because the motorway was so long and relentless and although I had no real choice I found I didn't really want to go any further.

Repeat the refrain: 'You bastard, you bastard. How could you how could you,' and a rousing verse of 'I gave you everything and you didn't give a damn, you just took what you wanted and then cast me off and now you're living in my lovely house with your younger woman, you chinless nerdy fool you chinless nerdy fool.'

And the rumble of tyres on the asphalt, or whatever it is this endless interminable road is made of, the rumble of tyres says, 'That chinless nerdy fool he did you wrong he did you wrong oooooh the chinless nerdy fool Rumble Rumble the bastard the bastard did you wrong . . . ' and then the whoosh of air past the car and the sometime slam of a gust of wind says, 'Let's try to forget it and mooooove on . . . mooooove on . . . '

And altogether, the rumble and the road and the gusting of the wind and the whooshing of the air, for a chorus of 'You bastard you bastard. How could you how could you . . . '

Junction 32 for Blackpool pleasure beach, a whirl of lights and colours and a Vekoma

Suspended Looping Roller Coaster and a Tetley teacup ride on which you will spin sombre circles thinking, 'Was anyone ever as wronged as I?'

ONLY FOR THE HAPPY says the sign beneath the junction, so you carry on.

'Bring some wellingtons,' said Cassandra White. 'Bring some warm clothes. Bring some waterproof clothes. Bring lots of pairs of socks.'

Bring a sopping sense of affliction. Bring a host of grievances weighing you down. Bring your deep longing for your comfortable house, all the mindless gadgets you relied upon. Bring your smashed-up sense of purpose.

The headlines at five o'clock, and now it's Junction 36 for the Western Lakes and I can see mountains ahead.

The road winds through villages called Beanthwaite and it winds past cottages in slate. It winds uphill and round tight corners, where the car leans like a ship on a keel. Everywhere are mountains, hard and serious. A lorry grinds and snorts ahead and slows me down. I have Cassandra White's notes in my left hand, with my right I spin the wheel. Her notes say, 'Carry on along this road, DON'T lose heart! It seems endless, when you don't

17

know where you're going. But you will arrive!'

I haven't the first clue where I am going. Or what will happen if I ever get there.

I take a right off the main road, onto a thin and winding country lane. The tyres rattle over a cattle grid. My teeth rattle in my head. Two slate barns, a few sheep lying on the road. The road rises and to the left is a deep valley, filled with trees and bracken. Everything is green and red, summer and autumn mixed together. I have travelled hundreds of miles and now everything is quiet. Only my thoughts continue in their manic twitter.

Lydie Lydie Lydie Lydie Lydie Lydie Lydie they twitter . . .

Unthanked unloved unwanted unthanked unloved unwanted . . .

WATCH OUT say Cassandra's notes — don't miss the turning off the road — and I slow down and find a small drive nearly obscured by low-hanging branches, and I judder along that until I come to the gate. PARK BY THE GATE says Cassandra. Don't drive any further unless you want to spend the next two months digging out your car.

YOU ARE HERE! WELCOME . . .

Welcome to White Farm.

Your uncertain future begins here.

4

Cassandra White is not a virtuous widow with her grizzled hair coiled into a bun. She does not wear a series of shapeless outfits in black, and she does not, ever, sit in a rocking chair surveying the scene with her rheumy eyes, saying, 'Before my dear Harry died . . . ' or 'In my day . . . '

She does not walk falteringly with a stick and she does not smell faintly of mildew.

She does not say 'Oh dearie me' when she stumbles.

In short, Cassandra White is not the delicate old lady I conjured as I read her advert.

Really there's very little way I could have expected her at all.

She is possibly the most beautiful woman I've ever seen. She is six feet tall and she has a shock of orange hair, blood orange setting-sun orange, and when she marched down the drive to greet me it was flaming like a furnace on her head. She appeared with a beacon above her, saying, 'Welcome, did you find it OK?' She shot me a brilliant smile, as I stumbled out with my bags. A charming twist to her mouth. As I stepped heavily into the knee-high mud, she took a bag and carried it. And all the way into her house she was like a tour guide, 'And this is where my grandfather built the second part of the house, and this is the oak outer door my parents put in, and this is where my mother used to keep her horses,' and the whole layer upon layer of her family history, 'and this is where my late husband always smashed his head, be careful now.'

She was like a country hostess who somehow remained oblivious to the fact that her country pile was really a dump.

Because it was clear, as soon as we went inside, that Cassandra White lived in the biggest dump I had ever seen. A dump beyond my worst imaginings. Not a small dump, not a cramped hovel by any means. There was plenty of this dump, room upon room, each one full of family heirlooms and mouldering clocks and sour old bits of furniture teetering on the ancient slate. There was the storeroom with dead meat hanging in rows and layers of home-made wine and jam and cheese and butter and barrels of home-made cider and the greenhouse and the toolshed and the cowshed, where there was a pile of straw and the lingering stink of a cow.

'My last remaining cow,' said Cassandra,

with an angry nod.

And the unspeakable grossness of the dry toilet or, as Cassandra called it, the thunderbox. I didn't know about that when I first arrived — Lord Jesus, how I didn't know about that, and how I was soon enlightened — but I did observe that the kitchen was a place of damp-ravaged tiles and peeling wallpaper, with the shrill high smell of rotting matter and something else, something even worse.

I somehow doubted — glancing around again — that Cassandra had anything like a dishwasher. I doubted she had a Magimix or a microwave. And there was no sign of a set of matching dishcloths and a range of oversized wine glasses and tasteful ranks of white crockery.

Indeed the inventory of Cassandra White's kitchen would read:

Three chipped cups and a stained teapot, relicts of an ancient tea set

A mound of detritus

Some mould

A double-barrelled shotgun

200 mice

Three rats

'Do have a cup of tea,' said Cassandra White, taking a kettle from the stove and pouring water into a pot.

There was some fruit on the table. She had a generous broad local accent and she said 'coop' for 'cup'. In her bony face shone her perfect teeth. Her cheekbones jutted beneath her sunken eyes, her skin was taut-translucent across her bones. Her eyes were green and they fixed on you, she just smiled and stared so finally I said, 'Well, thanks for inviting me over. I don't really know what I would have done otherwise.'

'You fell on hard times, did you?' she said.

'Yes, essentially.'

'Have a piece of fruit,' she said. 'It's from the garden. I don't have toast. I regard bread as a vice.'

'What, because it's a carbohydrate?' I said.

'No, because of grain. Grain is a hoarder's commodity. An appalling thing. You hoard it and then you create armies to protect you and your grain. You create big surveillance towers to watch the grain. Those ancient grain cities thousands of years before Christ, that's what happened to them. A big tower, full of soldiers, with an eye on the top, watching everyone.'

'Really? So because of the ancient cities you don't eat bread?'

'Because of the evil effects of grain in general.'

'OKAAAY,' I said, while thinking, *About*

TURN! QUICK MARCH! EVACUATE EVACUATE!

'I don't like much of what I see around me,' said Cassandra. 'So I live here and keep my head down, and try to fend for myself as much as I can.'

'How long have you lived here?'

'My family's owned this farm for hundreds of years. We've been in this valley for thousands of years, I reckon. My parents only had girl children, so I inherited the farm. I was the farmer and then when I married everyone called me the farmer's wife. My husband wasn't a farmer at all, though. He was in the army and he was blown up in the desert. Then foot-and-mouth destroyed this valley and when they had slaughtered all my cattle the government offered me two cheques. For my husband and for my cattle. I couldn't take either. So I sold most of my land. I've a couple of acres left. Everyone else took their cattle money and bought up my land and my farm fell apart.'

'I'm very sorry to hear it.'

'It's not important.'

'Of course it is. It's terrible.' And I was sorry for her. She lived in a slum and her husband had been blown across a desert. Then in a fit of pique she had shafted herself

23

entirely. It was hardly as if she was having a really fun time.

Her house felt as if a high wind would tear it to pieces, drive it back across the fields. On the stove a vat of water bubbled and steamed. 'I don't generate enough electricity for a kettle,' she said.

When I had finished my tea, she stood up and said, 'I'll show you around a bit.' So she marched me out of the kitchen into a draughty dining room, with a grand oak table and a few drunken chairs. A clock chiming in the background. A big portrait of a man in a frock coat.

'My great-grandfather,' said Cassandra. Glaring down at her, wondering what the hell she had done to his farm.

'Mmm,' I said, as my limbs ached with the cold. Then a frigid living room lurking under oppressive beams. Some armchairs with their stuffing spewed out. A big smelly rug. 'You have dogs?' I asked, already knowing the answer.

'Yes. They're in the yard,' said Cassandra.

'Great,' I lied. 'I love dogs,' I added as if I hadn't lied enough. She gleamed a smile and tossed her mane.

All the way up the stairs, her ancestors glared down at us, cold-faced and angry, and there were two more recent portraits, in pen and ink.

'Who are they?' I asked.

'My children,' she said. 'Jacob and Evelyn.'

'What do they do?'

'Oh, it's very sad, I love them dearly but they're both completely insane.'

'Are they in an institution?'

'Both of them, yes. Jacob is a management consultant in Sydney and Evelyn is a trader in New York. They don't talk to me any more.'

'But they have a history of mental illness?'

'No, no, that is their mental illness.'

'That they think they're a management consultant and a trader?'

'That they ARE a management consultant and a trader.'

'Okaaay,' I said.

We turned along a corridor and there was a bathroom with an ugly iron bath and a chipped sink and curiously enough no toilet, and some big cold bedrooms, each with a venerable bed, a few landscapes on the walls, their colours bleeding away, an oversized dressing table, some china.

'Fortunately for me this house was built to last,' said Cassandra. 'Keeps the rain off my head. Stops me freezing in the winter.'

'Charming,' I said.

Cassandra White has stripped her life of

frills and comfort. Her house is an unsettled pile of slate, neglected and shambolic. She doesn't even seem to notice. She holds her head high. Her arms are sinewy. Her shoulders are broad and padded with gristle. She has creases around her eyes, ingrained furrows from staring into the sun. She has still more lines drawn deep into her forehead. Her hair gets into her eyes and she blows it out again. She wears the same pair of old cords every day and the same blue jumper. She has a big pair of muddy wellingtons and a battered wax jacket. She stalks across her dwindled stretch of land and she grabs goats and hurls them around. Every day she works, to bring in water and light the fires and shovel shit and milk the goats and collect grey water or rainwater or whatever sort of water it is, just not mains water lest she be afflicted by plague or ebola or drugged and rendered compliant or whatever it is she's worried about.

We were almost friends but then she showed me the thunderbox. After that I couldn't forgive her for a long time. We were crossing a yard and before us was a little wooden hut with a door halfway up it, and steps leading to the door. There were two chimneys coming out of the roof. In my naivety and optimism I thought, 'How delightful, perhaps I could use it as a study, a cosy little study where I will be able to pass the mornings reading,' and then as we approached I became aware of a strange musky fetid aroma coming from the place, a wafting earthly stink of matter, MATTER.

Disgusting, I thought. An outside toilet. How unnecessarily vile.

But this was no ordinary toilet.

This was a thunderbox.

A thunderbox, Cassandra White explained to me, was the invention of a man who was clearly insane. This man decided that there was simply no need to flush your shit away, and instead you could more naturally and more charmingly store it in a massive pile in a chamber under your toilet.

'It's absurd that we use animal manure but not human manure. It's just squeamishness, we don't want to accept that we are also beasts. Anyway flushing your waste pollutes available drinking water and also wastes all the nutrients within the waste,' said Cassandra.

'It also stops it sitting in a big pile under your toilet,' I said.

'That just dries out the waste and then every so often you pat down the pile of waste under the toilet. It's a two-chamber system so eventually you transfer to the second chamber so the first chamber can compost down. That takes years though, as long as you pat down the pile. It's not as if you're shovelling it out every weekend. Then eventually when it's all composted you put it round the fruit trees in the garden.'

'You actually put it on your garden?' I said, thinking of the fruit I'd just eaten.

'Of course. It's great compost. Anyway obviously there are some different rules with a thunderbox so it's best if you don't piss down the toilet, piss is no good to anyone, so piss in this bucket instead, and don't put too much paper in the thunderbox, and always pour some sawdust down after you've finished, and close the lid afterwards, so you don't get flies in there. Flies love the damn thing, of course. I also put a lot of waste from the kitchen and garden down there, just to keep it all moving along.'

For a moment I thought she was toying with me, and there was actually another toilet elsewhere, a whopping toilet with a lovely whopping flush, whisking everything away before you could say 'Crapper'. But no, it turned out there really was this thunderbox and a bucket and a shovel, and a set of rules which made my stomach turn and do a crazy waltz just to read them.

It's curious how the presence of such a

28

thing, such a phenomenon, causes you to think anew about everything. Certainly it made me regard Cassandra as a dangerous coprophiliac who had dragged me into her lair. Certainly I sat down to dinner feeling sick and sorry for myself.

The fact of the thunderbox, its existence as a material object only a few metres away from me, well nigh ruined my meal, which was a hearty wood pigeon with some weird substance called quinoa and home-grown spaghetti marrows and chard, and a hunk of goat's cheese from one of Cassandra's obliging beasts. We ate it in the dining room, where the chairs were so rickety it was as if Cassandra had sawn their legs off unevenly, deliberately to sabotage them.

As we ate Cassandra offered a few helpful maxims, thus: 'Quinoa is a gift to the brain. It is a brain food, it amplifies the power of the brain.' Or 'Everyone is trying to convince you you're wrong in your instincts. But what if your instincts are right?' Or 'Nobody knows anything about anything in the end. So you may as well make up a reality and stick to it. At least then you're not being buffeted around by other people's nonsense.'

And I nodded.

When she had finished and pushed back

her plate she said, 'You lived in a nice big house?'

'Yes, pretty big.'

'In a nice part of town?'

'Yes.'

'Handsome husband?'

'Well, not too bad.'

'So what went wrong?'

'Oh, it was a mutual decision.'

'He ran off with someone else?'

'Yes, if you must know.'

'Well, that was bad luck.'

'We had fertility issues.'

'What, you couldn't get banged up?'

'No.'

'Were you the pampered housewife?'

'No, I had a job.'

'What job?'

'I worked in an office.'

'An office? What did you do there?'

'Oh, I was a project manager for a multinational corporation,' I said.

'Really, did you have a desk all of your own? A nice view of the car park? Your very own in-tray and your very own out-tray?'

'It wasn't like that,' I said, even though it was.

There was a pause, then I said, 'So have you been here all your life? Did you go away to university at all?'

30

That made her so scornful she nearly curled her lip.

'Why on earth would I have done that?'

'Well, for a change. To learn something.'

'What, to learn a load of sanctioned facts? Some nonsensical syllabus cooked up to lie to us all? To bow to a canon of learned bores talking undiluted madness?'

'You just sound as if you went to university,' I said.

It turns out Cassandra White is opposed to all formal education. If it was up to her we would all run riot in the fields and entertain ourselves building dens in the straw. Then we would read with our parents in the evening. We would be given a telescope and told to look at the stars. We would be taught how to identify fruits and vegetables and trees and plants. We would learn by inclination and necessity. We would never be stymied by the evils of a syllabus. In the world of Cassandra White to be a history teacher is like being a drugs dealer.

'They traffic in fake facts. They buy and sell lies. They are lie-mongerers,' she said.

Cassandra White is a woman made of bone and wire, stern green eyes, flame-red hair, strong shoulders. In a sense I admired her, as I shuddered away in her dining room, for having rigged up all her windmills or waterwheels or whatever she had; I thought it was truly slap-on-the-back wonderful that she was doing it, but I also thought that a few days of this life would probably kill me. I am after all the fleshly spoils of the suburbs, and if I exercise it is in a smart tracksuit in a gym, with the knowledge that a relaxing sauna awaits me when I stumble away from my exercise machine. And if I freeze it is outside and expecting that inside I shall be warm.

With the physical and doubtless psychological gulf opening up between us, I didn't think I would be much help to Cassandra White, and aside from such warm and courteous thoughts I could see it would be a major hassle and deep in my innermost core I just couldn't be bothered.

After dinner we sat in the living room and Cassandra threw a few logs onto the fire, and that made the place just above freezing, and she had some newspapers — 'Micklethwaite gave me these to light my fire with,' she said. 'I don't buy them myself.' As she tore them into pieces she read out a headline or two: 'Parents of abducted child are now suspects, say police.' 'Leading businessman convicted of downloading hardcore child pornography.' 'Internet communities infiltrated by paedophiles.'

'Strange, aren't they?' she said, throwing the scraps onto the fire.

'It's just the usual news.'

'But isn't it curious that there are so many stories about paedophilia?'

'Well, it's in the public interest.'

'But why is the public so interested?'

'Well, it's a shocking crime.'

'But this obsessive interest gets a bit weird, don't you think?'

'In what way?'

'Almost as if people are so very interested because they are in fact paedophiles themselves?'

'I hardly think everyone is a paedophile simply because they read stories about paedophilia.'

'They don't just read them. They hunt them out. They love them. They're like Victorians condemning prostitution. Ooh, terrible, tell me more, so I can get really outraged. Ooh, that's dreadful, I must hear more so I understand precisely the nature of this pure evil.'

'That's nonsense.'

'Rubbing their hands.'

'No they're not.'

'Oh, but they are. Rubbing their sweaty little palms.'

Aside from this proposal, Cassandra also

spent our first evening together explaining the following to me:

The government is full of fat fools in suits who have been cosseted for so long they have no idea about real life.

The government tells us what to eat and what to drink and how we must be healthy and then whenever there's a big company wanting to kill us with alcohol or sugar or GM foods, the government waves it through and lets us all be poisoned.

The government is interchangeable and each member of the government tumbles into some eternally allotted archetypal role of corruption and evil compromise and the idea of every system of top-down government is to force us all into equally eternal archetypes which stymie our potential . . .

The only thing to do is head for the hills.

'Preferably with a big blunderbuss,' she added. Then she yawned and said, 'Well, I'm hitting the sack.'

The first night I couldn't sleep in the cold bed with the inevitable lumpy hard-as-bone mattress and the window banging with every gale-force blast. I squeezed myself into a ball and screwed my eyes shut, and I lay there begging myself to sleep. Then I rolled over and tried on the other side. Hips aching, and all the time I was trying to think of a plan.

There was some beaten clock ticking in the corner of the room, tick tock tick tock and I thought of Cassandra in her lonely bed, her six-foot frame arranged to fill the space left by her husband, this husband she lost to some preposterous war, miles away in a place she had never been. It was bad, of course, but it wasn't my problem. If she wanted to stage her own personal decline then that was fair enough, if she found it helped, but I was relatively young and still had some grip on reality and didn't have to join in.

Besides, I've never enjoyed slumming it. There are people who go on holiday and stay in youth hostels or grimy B-and-Bs and listen to people snoring in the next room and they don't mind. They even like it. Some people don't have any choice, but I mean people who have a choice and choose it all the same.

I hate that sort of thing. I hate being cold or uncomfortable. I hate having to think about my greedy demanding body. I just like to service it and then forget it.

So I lay there for a few more hours shivering and fantasising about a sauna or a hot tub. I thought about ladling hot water onto my head and thawing my limbs through. Then the birds started chirping outside and dawn broke. The curtains were hanging off the rail and let in all the light anyway.

I got up. I shuddered until I had put on all my clothes. I wrapped my coat around my shoulders and went down the stairs, hoping not to see my hostess. I walked through the cavernous dining room and into the kitchen, where the stove was already lit. Cassandra wasn't around. It looked as if she was up already, which made me nervous. I went outside and thought I'd take a walk and then come back and tell her I couldn't do it. She wouldn't be surprised. She already thought I was lily-livered office scum.

I squelched through the mud and manure and pushed open the gate. At the drive I found a track which looked as if it went up a hill. So I walked along that and it wound up and up and passed another farm, this one clean and prim in the early light. I kept climbing because it made me sweat and it was a plain relief not to be shuddering in a deep frozen bed. There were sheep on the path and bracken rustled under my feet, autumn bracken in stunted red. I kept on climbing and didn't look back so when I'd panted to the top I turned and saw the valley for the first time spread out beneath me, and for all my malaise it was purely beautiful. It looked so old and many coloured, with the early sun rising on one side and the clouds casting their shadows all along it. And the rise and fall of the mountains, and the trees with their faded orange leaves. It made me think again. I thought, the thing is, I have nowhere else to go.

But remember the house is a slum, some small voice of reason said within my head.

And it was impossible to ignore, the undeniable fact of the house being a stinking crap heap.

So what are you waiting for?

I don't want to let her down.

What are you talking about? The voice of reason, now writhing in disbelief. *She's far too nuts to even notice if you leave.*

Well, that's probably just bluster. She's most likely lonely. Anyway . . . there's this view . . .

The view — who the hell cares about a view? Are you listening? Who gives a damn about a view? Are you going to take a bath in your view? Are you going to stave off hypothermia with the view? Remember how cold it is in that house. And it's only October. Winter's coming. It'll get much worse. You'll die in there.

But otherwise what do I do? I can't go back. I can't go into reverse.

You go into reverse if you want to. Back to the nice quiet office. The nice warm office. Rent a little flat. You'll be just fine.

But is it enough to be just fine? Is that enough?

Yes. Yes, it is enough. It ought to be enough. Just what is it you're trying to do, ruin everything?

The unedifying truth is that it turns out I am a parasite.

I wanted to suck up Cassandra's rich and foaming sense of purpose. And perhaps I didn't want to admit I had made a terrible mistake. Or worse still I might just have been too embarrassed to tell her I wanted to go. I ended up staying anyway.

5

So Cassandra told me what I needed to know. It was something like:

1. Thou shalt not receive electricity from the national grid. Instead thou shalt establish a wind turbine and a waterwheel, and also thou shalt use gas lights and candles and thy lights will glow sullen and sallow and thou shalt squint to see in the evenings and go to bed at 9:00 p.m.
2. Thou shalt not receive water from the Water Board, instead thou shalt take water from the stream. As a result thou shalt never really have enough water for anything and shalt spend three hours trying to have a bath.
3. Thou shalt chop wood for the fires and oven and break thy back carrying it into the house and stuffing it into the stove.
4. Thou shalt drink cow's milk from thy one remaining cow, Daphne, and goat's milk from thy saggy old goats and eat eggs from thy screeching hens and take bits of game from some ropy local

poacher, and thou shalt have a few pigs snorting around in the dirt on a scabby patch of land, and from time to time thou shalt massacre one or two of them for meat and thou shalt grow thine own vegetables and generally never part with any money nor eat anything thou art not personally responsible for.

5. Thou shalt send any officials who try to regulate thy various activities away from thy house with a flea really hopping in their ear, and thou shalt make all the neighbours rumble away about what a battleaxe thou hast become since thy husband died.

And of course

6. Thou shalt not eat bread because grain is the oppressor's food.

Then she explained some other things, i.e. that democracy is a terrible lie, that Darwinism is simply not true, that no one knows anything about the real origins of the species and that there was probably once a highly advanced civilisation on the planet which was completely wiped out and left no trace because it was so very civilised and advanced that it got along only using wood and wind and solar power, and we have not been progressing in a glorious teleology since the beginning of time but are probably relatively simple and backward compared to such tragically lost civilisations that have at various unknown points existed on the planet. And that cancer is an invention of modern life because we are all poisoned by the environment, which is riddled with chemicals and gamma rays and other 'really ridiculously bad crap'.

Cassandra explained all this to me very patiently, so that we could get it clear from the start, she said. After this she hoped I would just get on with things because, she added, she had a load of work to do and couldn't keep explaining things to me which really if I had any wit at all I should be able to pick up immediately.

So once she had said all that she spent the rest of the day barking orders at me and barely explaining anything at all.

* * *

'Fetch water.'

'Where do I fetch it from?'

'Look around you. Find some water. Then fetch it.'

*　*　*

'Fetch wood.'
  'Where do I fetch it from?'
  'The wood, of course.'
  'What do I fetch it with?'
  'Well, there are various techniques you could use including asking the trees to give up their branches and begging the branches to walk along behind you, but I would suggest a bloody big axe and a basket.'

*　*　*

'Collect some potatoes from the vegetable patch.'

*　*　*

'Bring in the turnips and swedes and parsnips and put them into storage.'

*　*　*

And I began to think that what she was really saying was:
  Atone for your previous life.
  Yes, go and damn well atone for it.
  So I went off to get the water and to fetch the wood and my decadent soul was thinking

but this is really hard work and I don't like this one bit. Why is this what I end up doing? Why this?

'Only that?' said Cassandra some hours later, looking into the basket. 'Only that to show for three hours with an axe?'

'It's my first time,' I said.

'In a forest?'

'In a forest with an axe.'

She snorted and turned away.

All my life I've avoided manual work. If possible I have paid others to do the sweaty menial tasks I didn't want to do. Unblocking the drains. Fixing the electrics. Mending the washing machine. I assumed I wouldn't enjoy them, though naturally I never bothered to find out by actually trying.

I don't think I'm alone in never having brought in my own wood or drawn my own water in heavy sloshing buckets from a well.

That's the deal with the twenty-first century. You run the risks of obesity and being killed in a car crash, but you don't have to worry about hurrying through the forests with a spear and lugging an animal carcass home. You pay a cleaner to shove a Hoover around your house and you certainly never do the real sinew-tugging work, like dragging a massive log across a forest floor and smashing it into pieces or man-hauling a pig around its native mud slide or hammering sheets of metal.

It turns out that for Cassandra these are barely noticeable necessary acts.

'Only that?' she said, when I came back with another basket of wood.

'Still only that?'

Only this, my shabby unused limbs. Only my unused sinews, already in outraged spasms. Only my unfit frame, bent under the unaccustomed burden.

And I remembered — dimly, as if that life was fading fast from my head — how I had a wood burner, a really nice wood burner in my living room.

It was filled with uniformly proportioned bits of wood, which I had delivered by a man called Keith.

Keith dragged all the wood in and left it in the tasteful wood basket I had positioned by the fire. I would feel genuinely affronted if Keith dropped any bits of bark or branches on the living-room carpet. There was the immaculate inside of my house and there was the dirt-strewn outside — the street, the garden, the land in general — and if it was necessary to have some wood brought inside then I wanted it kept in the damn wood basket.

My involvement was confined to — at a

later stage — taking a piece of wood between some brass tongs and, oh it was hard, shoving it into the wood burner.

Occasionally, perhaps, I threw away a chunk of wood which hadn't really burned. Yes, I really did that, I really took it into the garden and threw it into the shrubbery.

After a few hours of grunting my throat hoarse in the vegetable patch, and feeling my vertebrae decaying even as I bent double over a spade, I said to Cassandra that I thought growing your own vegetables might be a lot of unnecessary work, when there were so many nice vegetables around and even in the supermarket.

That made her really spit blood, and she said, 'If you buy food from a supermarket you are part of a process in which farmers are nailed. Farmers are nailed, and then you're destroying the planet anyway because your food has been flown thousands of miles and is wrapped in a thousand yards of plastic and all this crazy packaging you throw away as soon as you get home. And why is it packaged like that? So that it stays so-called fresh on the shelves, so that it remains just about edible even after it's been sweated under the lights for days and days. And as it sweats all this weird stuff in the plastic gets warmed into life and seeps into the food and then you buy it thinking mmm that looks nice and fresh. Radiated plastic, that's what you're eating.'

Go and sweat in the garden instead, she said. Go and break your back dragging in a few turnips. Get some turnips, get some twisted and stunted and unappetisingly natural turnips and then get some rancid insect nibbled salads and there! A tasty lunch, she said.

'Mmm,' I said.

Mud and turnips. Mud under your nails. Mud in your hair. And a stink of mud which lingers on you, which permeates your every pore and becomes inescapable. It becomes you. You came from mud and it is to mud that you will return and each day you wallow in mud and mud is you.

Mud and its deep dark companion, manure.

I was thinking of my old neglected garden, with the decaying apple tree I never harvested and the thousand plants I never cared for. I just left old Cyril to tend to them, and on hot days I lay on the patio on a deckchair, wearing a hat and slapping sun lotion on my pasty limbs.

I said, 'Oh, thanks so much, Cyril, it's looking simply marvellous,' and I handed him his wages in an envelope. My neat envelope into his muddy hands. 'Oh see you next week,

46

Cyril, you obedient serving man, and perhaps you'll hoe the borders when you come.' Doff the cap, went Cyril, thanks so much for letting me pull up your weeds. I liked to look at the neat garden, the neat arrangements of purple and orange, the flowers I had ordered Cyril to plant. I stared down at it, pleased by its orderliness, but I hardly even touched the grass.

Oh I ate well at home. I liked to cook. I even prided myself on my dinner parties. I would drive off to a big fat supermarket and wheel a trolley down the aisles. Piling the stuff in, all those packages. I would take all my plastic home and then I would cook everything up, and everyone always liked it.

'Amazing soup,' my guests would say. 'How on earth did you make it?'

'You trashed the earth,' said Cassandra. 'That's how you made it.'

6

So I am tugging at a goat's dug. It's Monday morning and it's so early that my eyes are still half shut. I have a smelly old goat's dug in my hand, and I'm tugging at it in a harsh and insensitive way, and the goat seems even unhappier about this state of affairs than I am. There's nothing coming out of this dug, for all my urgent tugging.

Even if I could open my eyes I'm not sure I would.

It's Monday and when I've finished with the goat I follow Cassandra around holding bits of straw and trying not to look or breathe as she shovels great piles of chicken shit into a bag.

'Good manure,' she says.

At the vegetable garden she shows me how she irrigates the land with some complicated rainwater drainage system and then she shows me how to sow broad beans. There are neat lines of vegetables, and I observe that if Cassandra's house is an unruly slum then she certainly knows how to keep a tidy vegetable patch. She bends her scrawniness, pushes back her beacon hair, and says, 'OK you stay here and get some artichokes and carrots in, if you don't mind.' The 'if you don't mind' is plainly satirical. I have no choice, and anyway it keeps me warm.

The chickens are fed and Cassandra goes off to do something with the pigs and after that she is gone for hours. I stumble around the vegetable patch under orders, dragging vegetables out of the soil. The dirt gets under my fingernails and I often swear. I emit flurries of swearing but to no one, to the cold grey sky and the stink of the muck.

Tuesday, after the morning milking when my reluctant goat releases as scanty a trickle of milk as the day before, we go off to rebuild the rabbit fence. We pick away at bits of wire and re-thread them and we set mouse traps. I fall in the mud and Cassandra laughs, cruelly and uproariously, abandoned to the riotous comedy and then she says, 'I'm so sorry, that was awful of me. Why don't you go home and have a bath?'

I spend some time heating up water on the stove and carrying it upstairs and tipping it into the bath, thinking well at least this can't be too bad, a nice hot bath, but by the time I've enough water for a bath the earlier water has been chilled by the underlying froideur of the house and I sit in tepid muddy water thinking, 'How lovely, how relaxing.'

I put on my jeans, which I left on the floor in my bedroom, and after I have been wearing them for a few minutes I feel a sharp pricking at the top of my thigh, just by my pants. 'Strange,' I think. 'As if there's a pin in my pocket.' But I know there isn't a pin in my pocket so I go downstairs and make myself a cup of tea.

In the kitchen I feel the pricking again, and it's even harder and more pin-like this time, and I think, 'Could I have accidentally put a pin in my pocket without realising it?' So I feel in my pocket for a pin but can't find anything. Then I get pricked really sharply and inescapably, so I push my trousers down to my knees and feel around. I can't find any pins and just as I am about to accept defeat I see the source of my discomfort.

Oh yes, I see the source — a vast black beetle, a beetle so vast and black and shiny and so blatantly waving his limbs around and burrowing towards my flesh to dig his little pincers in again, that I begin to scream and dance around, trying to leap out of my trousers but tangled in the cloth, kicking them away from me and nearly falling, and when I've got them off I stand in my pants in the frozen kitchen, screaming.

The beetle limps out of my trousers and crawls off wearily to die.

I drink my tea, shocked and even angry with the beetle for crawling into my pants, and then I feel a vague sense of guilt about it being so mangled by the end and perhaps even missing a leg, but then how was I to know it had decided to set up camp in my trousers? How was I to know, I think, about the tragic error the beetle had made, its fatally unwise choice of accommodation?

I go outside again and as if nature is avenging the death of an innocent if foolish beetle it pisses rain onto my head as I drag a goat along on its rope and eventually the goat kicks and I fall into the mud again.

★ ★ ★

I mention the bath to Cassandra over dinner — keeping quiet about the beetle nonetheless — and I ask how she gets it hot and she laughs and says, 'I bathe very rarely.'

'How do you wash then?'

'I've never really understood the contemporary fetish about washing.'

'It's not a fetish, I would just like to do it occasionally, especially if I spend the days tumbling around in chicken shit.'

'Why do you think it's better to be covered in fat than in chicken shit?'

'The bath does not cover me in fat.'

'Of course it does. You're lathering yourself up with sodium tallowate, which comes from beef fat. So your skin is covered in beef fat and you think you're clean.'

'Well, soap smells better than shit.'

'Only because it's full of chemical perfumes.'

'No, because it is not shit.'

'Essentially it's worse than shit.'

'So you don't bathe at all?'

'In the summer when I sweat more I swim every evening in the river. In the winter it's not so important. A quick splash every so often. No need to be a fetishist, rubbing every pore with a big handful of fat.'

Just get down in the mud and work.

In the mud. Yes, that bit of mud. Get into it.

Then work.

★ ★ ★

It's not even light. Dawn hasn't even broken and there's the sound of clattering in the kitchen. The birds aren't even singing in the trees. There's no sign of life except Cassandra.

Arise! The scrappy remnants of the farm await thy labours!

Work! Work! WORK! Hold your hoe and

wave it in a conspicuously useless way.

Sleep! Because tomorrow the scrappy remnants of the farm await thy labours!

There's the damn goat field and the damn pig house and the cow patch and then there's a small orchard, all Cassandra's shit-fuelled fruit trees, and beyond the trees are some chickens in their chicken pen, a proper little avian Eden with a tree and a nesting box and a wooden house. Then a small pond with some ducks honking around it.

Beyond that there's a line of beehives with a nasty buzzing pile of bees. 'The only sugar I eat is honey,' says Cassandra. 'You don't need anything else. There was no sugar in the average diet in Britain until the eighteenth century. We're not designed to tank ourselves up on sugar. It confuses the body and gives it the wrong idea.'

'Wrong idea about what?'

'About life.'

In her garden Cassandra grows cabbages and kale, artichokes, broccoli, swedes, cauliflower, Brussels sprouts, potatoes . . . Runner beans, peas, broad beans, French beans, spinach, lettuce, celery, leeks, onions, mangolds, whatever on God's earth they are, beetroot, herbs, rhubarb, raspberries, marrows. And lots of other things.

She lists it as we walk around, like a

mantra. Eventually she says I too will know it and then I will have discovered the truth beneath the gauze of untruth, the realities inherent if we could only but perceive them . . .

★   ★   ★

Arise! There is a frigid day dawning, the cold land awaits you.

Work! Work! Grip a spade between your frosted fingers and pound the soil, and drag your nails in the dirt as the rain slaps your face.

Sleep! Sleep as if you have been drugged, the weight of your exhaustion dragging you under.

The first biting sniff of cold in the morning. Then there's the stink of the thunderbox, oh the stink of the thunderbox that makes you dread the call of nature. You struggle against it, how you struggle not to heed it but you are called nonetheless. Summoned to the stink.

The smell of wood burning in the stove and the fine clean smell of tea. That sustains me for a while, and then it's out to the stinking yard, the stink of goats and chicken muck and the smell in my hands and hair, the smell of simple ordure, matter, filth, entirely inescapable, so deep in my nostrils I think I have swallowed it, that I have supped on chicken shit and drunk deep of liquid crap.

The smell of goat milk, rich and phlegmy, and the smell of the goat's skin and its dirty old dug in my hand.

Breathe in breathe in and now the smell of mulch, the straw and bark Cassandra scatters on the garden, the smell of this mulch slowly rotting. And exhale and now mmmm lovely inhale the smell of manure on another patch of ground . . . mmmm decay and earth . . . inhale . . . exhale . . . and a blast of dung as I pass through the cow patch mmmm . . . and the smell of rainwater and flowers and vegetables, as I move from row to row, the vegetables giving up their smells — mmmm . . . And woodsmoke rising and dispersing.

We make cheese — or I watch Cassandra — and that is a fatty rich smell which squats in my nostrils, an overpowering smell of curdled milk, and the smell of whey, a thin and tepid smell.

And the stink of the store where the cider barrels are, a deep smell of fruit turned yeasty and fermented.

The sweet smell of Cassandra's home-made rhubarb wine.

The slow burn of wax as the evening

candles flare and sputter.

The evening farewell stink of the thunder-box, blasting me to bed.

And all these smells gather on my skin and in my hair and linger through the day, and however much I wash I always smell mulch and matter on my hands and the stink of earth and rot in my hair.

On Wednesday we milk the goats, and my goat is still a stingy milk-free beast. Cassandra meanwhile is finished with her milking in a few minutes, and then she gives my goat a brisk tug to show me how it's done. The dug spills forth milk, and Cassandra says, 'She just has to get used to you. Takes about a week, usually.' Meanwhile old Daphne is releasing torrents of milk, pouring the stuff into a pail and for a moment I greedily covet the cow, I think my entire life would be transformed if I could only get to seize her dug, but Cassandra seems to want her for herself.

I clean up leaves from the vegetable garden, and hoe and weed, and dig plots and under strict instructions I lift out sundry root vegetables and put them into sand for storage.

Casandra shows me the 'drying room' as she calls it, which makes me naturally enough imagine clothes and a tumble dryer but is actually full of what look like dead bats hanging from ropes slung across the room.

'What the hell are they?' I say.

'They are going to be cigars.'

'You make cigars from dead bats?'

She laughs. 'They're tobacco leaves. Finest Cuban. I've been growing them for years and I've now developed this super-resilient variety, perfect for the Lake District. Cumbrian-Cuban cigars.'

'Isn't it completely illegal to grow your own tobacco?'

'Yes, under some madly punitive archaic act it is indeed entirely illegal. I'll roll you one later, you'll find they're quite tasty. At first they were really vile and I positively had to force myself to smoke them but I've refined them over the years.'

Later she gives me one and as I cough out chunks of lung I think that if these are her refined cigars then I am only glad I never tried the earlier ones.

Thursday we make jam. The kitchen is full of the stink of boiling fruit and clouds of steam rise from the pans. Then because we have used so much fuel boiling up the fruit Cassandra says I should go and get some more wood from the trees beyond the east fence, and sends me off with a saw and an axe.

When I return with a basketful of wood and my hands burning from the cold she tells me to stack it in the woodshed and make sure I shut the door firmly, so I go off muttering and slam the wood into piles and all the time my hands are throbbing as if I've hit them repeatedly with a mallet.

Then I try to walk to the village post office, and on the way I see an ancient farmer on a mini-tractor, chugging over the bridge. I aim at a friendly nod and he stares hard at me, neither smiling nor frowning, and carries on.

Friday oh let there be a grand chorus of hallelujah my goat dug releases a trail of milk, and finally the goat and I have reached an understanding.

'Good,' says Cassandra. 'I've never liked those goats. If you could milk them each day that would be perfect. Eventually you can do Daphne too.' And then my cup will surely runneth over.

Buoyed by my grand success I plead for time off and drive into the nearest town. The town looks bombed and blasted, though you can smell the sea and there are gulls circling above.

I go to a big grim shop and buy some jumpers and a big jacket and some thermal underwear and a lot of pairs of socks, and some sturdy walking boots and Wellingtons and a big soft duvet and a sleeping bag, and a hot-water bottle and a secret supply of hot chocolate, and a load of biscuits, which I will stash in my room in case Cassandra disapproves of such idle consumption of processed sugar.

When I return I'm relieved to discover she's in the fields, so I race up to my room with my spoils, and hide as many of them as I can in the cupboard. I put the duvet on my bed and stand there admiring it, feeling much better.

★　★　★

Saturday Cassandra has a rabbit which someone from the village has given her and she says, 'Why don't you cook it? Can you cook a rabbit?' and I say, 'Yes, I can cook a rabbit,' but then I see the creature and it's a whole rabbit, head and paws and all, and I hesitate.

'Come on now,' says Cassandra, as I back away from the still-warm rabbit. 'Don't be a weed. Here we go — I'll take out the guts for you.' And she does something revolting with a knife and there are guts everywhere.

'Now, here's the knife. Chop off its paws.'

'Oh God, I can't,' I say, looking at this little

bunny with its sad dead eyes and its belly all slashed.

'Just chop its paws off and stop making a fuss.' She is trying to hand me the knife but I won't take it.

'Can't you chop it up, and I'll cook it?' I say.

'It's easy. Look, get the paw here and just cut it like this' — and there it is, a paw. A poor little bloody rabbit's paw.

'Now you do the other one.'

'Really, now you've started can't you just . . .'

'You'll never learn otherwise.'

'I don't want to learn how to dismember a rabbit.'

'Ridiculous. Look — whack, whack whack, there you are' — and she chucks the pawless rabbit at me.

'Now chop off its head,' she says.

★ ★ ★

Cassandra goes out to get something from the next village and I wander into her bedroom — or rather I stand in the doorway of her bedroom, not wanting to venture further in case she's set some paranoiac's trap. I see her hard-as-nails bed with the iron bedstead, all lopsided and sloping away from the wall, and her bedside table filled with photographs of her husband — I assume. A tall man, a straight-backed military man, smiling at successive cameras. There's another on the wall, a big portrait, in uniform.

There's hardly anything else in the room, just a big teak cupboard. But every surface has photos in frames, even the windowsill, where they've curled and yellowed with the damp. I feel a sort of pity for her, that beneath her hard carapace there's a torn and ragged human, I expect, though that's all buried well enough. Locked in a sealed box, sunk a thousand leagues beneath. From the pictures I understand that Cassandra is deep in grief, perhaps insane with it, even now, more than a decade on.

I wonder if it's grief that has made her so tough and commanding, the need to marshal herself or be lost altogether. But her patchwork of ideas, her random outpourings, the bedraggled fundaments of her creed, the creed of being Cassandra White — I don't quite know where that came from.

* * *

We eat rabbit stew, with marrows and spinach leaves I have gathered from the garden.

Cassandra says, 'The best egg-laying breeds of chickens, well there are so many to choose from. The Rhode Island Red isn't bad at all — hardy, gives you big brown eggs. Or the White Leghorn, not bad either, decent white eggs. I like a nice white egg. What do you like, white or brown?'

'I don't really know,' I say.

'Now the Isa Brown,' she says, 'that's a bird that survives anything. You could drop them off a mountain in a blinding storm, you'd probably find them in the chicken coop the next day, looking the same as ever. You could blow those little freaks up with gelignite. They wouldn't notice. Decent eggs, nothing amazing. But good enough if you want a bird that can hack it.'

As we take the plates back to the kitchen she says, wistfully, poetically, 'I'd really like to have more cows again. Perhaps I can borrow a field. I'll get old Daphne breeding a bit. I miss making my own oxtail soup.'

'How do you make that?' I say, conversationally.

'Oh, it's quite easy. When you're slaughtering the cow you cut into the tail right near the arse and then you drag the tail out of its skin. Then you throw it in a pot.'

I don't even bother to respond.

62

* * *

The weather is relentlessly cold, taunting me each morning, but I curl up at night in the duvet and think I might just manage it, a few more weeks, a month or two, and then I can explain to Cassandra that I have to go back to my job.

I must go back to my job, I think.

My in-tray will be overflowing. So many things to audit and process.

I imagine the office, the neon lights, the purr of the heating, the round robins and the ceaseless variety of futile meetings.

The feeling of your elbows going numb as you type nonsense onto the screen.

RSI would be a release. They'd have to sign you off.

Oh merciful Lord please bless me with RSI. Please let me experience a terrible agony each time I lift my hands to the keyboard. Please let me weep as I explain to my boss that I can no longer type his memos, though they have thrilled me for many years.

Oh, how they have thrilled me . . .

And your silent prayer goes unanswered.

No RSI for you, you sinner. You have sinned too greatly, in your cubicle every day.

Daydreaming and wasting your time.

★　★　★

Arise! The steely will of Cassandra White awaits you.

Work! Work! Or you will sink into the cold earth and most likely die.

Sleep! Sleep deeply and in your dreams you will not be here; you will be warm and back in your previous life, a life which now seems like a dream itself . . .

It is impossible to get warm, unless you are bent double in the garden and clearly killing yourself slowly. In the house you are never warm. You are never quite comfortable.

Your throat itches from all the wood smoke. Your skin cracks with the dried-out chilled air. You rise aching from a night spent squirming in the lumpy bed.

You are never rested.

The food is good but then you are hungry half an hour later, because you spend the whole day roaming around in the biting wind.

There are mice everywhere, and you see them scuttling around when you enter a room. They are brazen vermin, and they stand on the kitchen table and salute you.

'You,' they say. 'Only you? Well, what do you want? You good for nothing! You abject coward! What are you going to do about us?'

There are flies and spiders and insects of

64

all varieties, varieties you never imagined. Crawling out of every corner. Flapping at your face in the night. Creeping under the covers. The whole house brims with nature. There is a free flow of nature all around it. A force field. Only four leaning shabby walls separate you from the cold black night and the rain-drenched hills.

★   ★   ★

Monday I dream of hot baths hot baths Tuesday I dream of cream cakes Wednesday I dream of my little cubicle, all safe and warm Thursday I dream of the sandwich girl with her evil mounds of devil's BREAD slathered with mayonnaise Friday I dream of a grand meeting in which I am standing in front of a whiteboard with a big fat marker pen and the boss is telling everyone just how well I've done. A big round of applause, for she who has done so well. And raise her up before you, for she is a good drone. Saturday I dream of love, someone who loves me and cares for me and Sunday I can't sleep for wondering what I have done.

And Cassandra says, 'No, you have to stack the wood in a pile like that. No not like that, like that.' That morning I simply think she is a tyrant, a bony-headed tyrant.

I am Sisyphus, or I am Sisyphus's less successful younger sister, who couldn't even get the rock halfway up the hill before it rumbled down again.

7

It must be masochism, or my judgement has slipped entirely. All the hours I squandered and the times I was idle and complacent and all the days I spent checking my email and waiting to go home, and all the times I ate fish and chips for dinner, and all the supermarket ready-made meals I shoved into my microwave, and all the ill-gotten electricity I used and my lifetime of unheeding and ordinary profligacy and now I am being punished.

Cassandra is the avenging angel I have summoned. I have brought her down upon my head.

And she is omniscient and without mercy. And her eyes gleam with righteousness. And she is the emissary of some deity I've never considered, but who I've enraged entirely.

An angry flame-headed deity, a deity spitting flame. Cassandra brings suffering and through suffering I will be healed. Though I know this is only what I deserve, I am weak and I resist the punishment. I gag on the medicine and I struggle against the lashes.

But they rain down anyway.

*   *   *

If she sees me relaxing by the fire with a good book, in the evening with all the marrows gathered, wood stacked, cheese curded, eggs collected and goats tethered, she sits down with me, lights one of her throat-scorching cigars and says, 'Why on earth are you reading that nonsense?'

'Because, you know, it's famous.'

'Wordsworth is a bastard.'

'Hardly,' I say. 'He's a famous landscape poet.'

'He's a bastard. He never did anything for the poor. He just wrote about how jolly they were, how they loved being poor and living in their hovels. Then he went home to his big house.'

'Dove Cottage wasn't very big. I went there once. It was rather . . . '

'The other one, Rydal Mount. The really big one.'

'Really? I haven't seen that one.'

'Don't bother, he's a bastard.'

When I bend down to the marrow patch and she to the potato rows, she says, 'In your house you were a pervert. You were a pervert for angled spotlights and halogen bulbs. That's why you were infertile. All your perversions sapped your body. Every time you

68

went to Ikea your fertility was further diminished. Every time you flicked through an interiors magazine and coveted a particular sort of tap for your newly renovated bathroom, your chi was smashed. Your body was constantly reeling from fresh assaults: the new lounge carpet. The brand new digitally timed oven. The flatscreen TV. The bath with inherent whirlpool. Smash, bang crash, suck suck suck, slurp, your life force ebbing away . . . '

'You constantly bought rubbish you didn't need and you stacked it all in your mad pervert castle.

'If you'd had a child you would have raised it to be a pervert too.'

She says, 'Your husband left you because he was either more of a pervert or less of a pervert than you. Only you can decide which.'

She says, 'All our perversions of yesteryear come to haunt us. You, a former queen of Pervert Manor, are being tormented by your perversity.'

Then there is a period of blissful silence and later she says, 'You're not an individual. You don't have an original thought in your head. You're not a self at all. You're just an adjunct of the great social being. Your self, this thing you think is a self is really just a tapestry of socially created ideas and anxieties. Even your anxieties, these things which make you unhappy, they're not really yours. You haven't thought them out at all.'

And I say, whipped and plaintive, 'So you're saying my feelings aren't real?'

'No, I'm saying nothing you think is original. You are just a concoction. There are millions and millions of people just like you. Perhaps we're all like you. Perhaps there's no such thing as a self, full stop.'

'How do you know? You never know what people are really thinking.'

'I do,' says Cassandra. 'I know exactly what you think about everything.'

★ ★ ★

'You should get more angry,' she tells me over dinner.

'I thought I was quite angry.'

'You're not at all angry. You think you deserved it. You think your barren womb drove your husband away. Have you ever considered the notion that it might have been him?'

'Him who drove himself away?'

'Him who was barren.'

'No, I never really thought of that.'

'Ridiculous. You let him blame you for everything.'

'I didn't.'

'Why are you here, living a life you hate, if you don't think you were to blame for everything?'

'I don't know.'

'Of course you don't know. It's far too complicated for your limited reserve of clichés. You can't understand yourself at all.'

'That's not true.'

'You should have shot him.'

'Who?'

'Your husband, of course. You should have got a shotgun and shot him in the arse.'

'I might have accidentally killed him.'

'Well, that wouldn't matter so much. There are plenty more weasels like him.'

'I don't really think he deserves to die.'

'Well, he deserves to die more than my husband did. My husband was a good man. A genuinely kind and generous man. Funny, patient, a wonderful man. And he got blown up and your weasel shit of a husband is still stalking the earth, enjoying himself.'

'It's very unfair.'

'Of course. But you don't need to sit around thinking it's all your fault.'

Cassandra pauses for a moment and then she says, 'The problem with you is that your brain is cram-full of other people's crap. You're like a septic tank that's never been cleaned. I'll take you out later and I'll show you the septic tank. That's what your brain looks like.'

★ ★ ★

This is how prisoners feel, I think. This is how people in a totalitarian state feel. They keep their chins in their collars. Head down, trying not to get smashed too hard.

Then she says, 'No no, not that. Don't do that. Or do it, but then impale yourself on the hoe afterwards. No no really that's not how you do it.'

Vengeance will be mine, I think, and I wonder about breaking the windows and dragging her through the fields. Vengeance will be mine soon, I think. And I put my head down and hurl the hoe around.

The neighbours are no consolation. Most of them nod grimly when I force them to acknowledge my presence, when I stand in front of them bellowing, 'HELLO' or 'Lovely weather'.

Even when the day is cold and conspicuously vile I bellow, 'Lovely weather,' at them all the same. Then there's a pause and then if I'm lucky they produce a reluctant nod. 'Fine shade of brown, the trees,' I offer.

Reluctant shrug, and maybe even a reluctant grunt. With that satisfying social exchange over, we go our separate ways.

Then there's the unsmiling farmer on his tractor, I see him every day when I go for my brief prisoner's exercise session across the bridge and up the road. He chugs past, staring me down. I am an unpaid labourer at White Farm and it's as if I am the untouchable of the village, Cassandra White's marrow slave, and no one must speak to me.

Yet there's a morning I'm on my own in the garden, having stepped outside into a gale wearing Wellington boots and squelched through undiluted muck to the hen coop to fish out some eggs.

Warm eggs, bits of straw clinging to them.

The cold biting at my hands.

My hands are chapped and torn. My face is burning under the wind. I'm cold and furious and wondering when this will end, and all I can think about are my chattering teeth and wet-through feet and the feeling of leather rubbing on a raw patch of my skin, and all the plain asperities of my state.

I stand up to ease my aching back and as I'm standing there rubbing my spine and thinking how I would like to grind Cassandra's face in the dirt I see the sun breaking through the clouds and sending a great shaft of light onto the side of a mountain, and all the trees suddenly clear and vibrant in the sunshine, and I feel something deep in my guts. What is it, this feeling in my guts? A sort of recognition? Awe? Nature lust?

In the places I have lived the stars have always been fading away, masked by the glow from streetlights. Here at night I gaze up at the heavens and they are scattered with thousands and thousands of stars.

The Milky Way is clear and plain above me, snaking and twirling in infinite space. Awe, in my miserable little brain, it seems incongruous, but there I am worshipping away.

Oh Mother Earth and the sun which rises and spreads some warmth upon my back even when the day is rigid and cold

Oh ancient fells steeped in reds and purples and the last vestiges of green

Oh river which trickles one day and then after a rainstorm flows in curdled yellow, like foaming beer

Oh stars, so many stars, I never understood just how many you were when most of you were wiped out by the glare of the town.

One day the valley shimmers under the sunshine and the next dark clouds gather. The rain stops and there are water droplets shining like diamonds on the leaves. You try to touch them and they vanish. The mountains are red and then they are sullen and grey. The sky changes all the time. You can never complain about the valley. It's constantly interesting, always shifting and rearranging itself. And here we are, in our ordinary gloom and me steeped in weariness but always on the move, dragging hoes and spades on my back, bent double with the weight of some implement, or crawling in the dirt, in search of food.

8

Then I get a postcard. It's a fine frigid day, the usual skin-cracking wind and uncertain threatening skies, and I am all ready for a day of being lashed by the cat-o'-nine-tails of Cassandra's condemnation, roasted on the spit for my many crimes, but when I get to the kitchen Cassandra is drinking tea and reading something.

A postcard.

I go in and pour some tea and after a minute she tosses the card over to me.

'Congratulations,' she says, not looking up.

I take the postcard and I read:

DEAREST — Lydie has gone. Please come back. I love you.

'You read this?' I say to Cassandra. 'But it's clearly private.'

'Well by the time I worked out who it was for, I'd got the basic thrust of it.'

I can't really imagine who on the planet would address Cassandra as dearest, but it seems heartless to point this out.

'Anyway, you must be delighted,' she says.

'You're free. You can go any time.'

I don't say anything, I just take the card and walk into the yard.

At first my only thought is LIBERTY! Then I entertain a big bold image of myself, packing all my things into the car and shrieking, 'FUCK YOU, WHITE' as I gun off down the drive. 'FUCK YOU and YOUR THUNDERBOX' I imagine myself yelling, and I am smirking as I stroll past the vile temple of matter itself and walk towards the duck pond clutching the card as if it is a winning lottery ticket. I am RELEASED, I think, and not a moment too soon. Another day and I might really have lost my grip. I might have descended and really found the mire.

I am walking to the sound of ducks quacking in their pond. (Pondlife according to Cassandra White: 'Of course you must keep the pond dirty. Dirt breeds life. Life is what ducks like. Ducks don't want a china gnome clutching a fishing rod. They want a stinking pond with lots of stuff in it.') The mulch laps at my feet, in a friendly way. ('Mmm, mulch, want to taste it? This is a fruity mulch, a fine rich resonant mulch, a sort of connoisseur's mulch, too refined for you.' Mulch according to Cassandra White.)

And there are the mangy old goats, gnawing the cold grass and the foolish ranks of chickens, pecking in the dirt, and there are the mountains mottled with light and shadow.

I am saved, I think.

Saved from the bent-backed grind of it. From the pressure in my head. The daily lashings. The clatter and smash of the windows in the night. The rising at dawn with nothing but the smell of cold around me.

I am saved, I think, and I aim at a joyful bound. I aim at something like a skip, a hop of grim-faced liberty.

I try, grim-faced and cold, to jump for joy.

Dearest.

I love you.

And I think of my presumptuous husband, dumped by his fantasy girl, perhaps a little heart-broken and now — out of some cowardly fear of being alone — penning his lazy, presumptuous postcard and shoving it in the post. He thinks a line is enough. Outrageous!

A scribbled summons, that'll do it, he thinks. He didn't even buy the postcard; it's one I bought a while ago from the local museum, a floral view. He hardly even glanced at it when he found it on a shelf. He just sent it off. Sat back and waited. Of course she'll come back, he's thinking. What else does she have?

But surely it's not so bad, I think, to live

with a husband you don't really love and do a job you despise. You get your rewards, I think.

You get your cosy cubicle and your weekly trip down the pub with your colleagues.

You get the office scapegoat, a sad man called Tim.

You get your warm house and your little car and you get to putter off to the shops and buy yourself clean new clothes straight from a mass-production line in China.

You get the television, the reassuring blur of noise and colour so you never have to contemplate the dense blackness in your head.

You don't have to stare into the blackness, shining a light into it shouting, 'Anything there? Anything at all?'

* * *

Dearest. If I'm honest I don't really love you, rather the thing is that I am afraid of being alone, and now that Lydie has gone I have realised what a deeply vacant soul I have, a soul lacking in any depth at all and I am frightened of the resounding silence of my empty being . . . Frankly my darling you are the only option left.

* * *

Now I walk slowly in the sunshine with the birds twittering in the trees and some pigeons doing their crazy circles above the garden.

I imagine getting in the car and driving off. All the way down the M6 again.

White Farm receding into the distance, the smell fading from my clothes and hands.

Arriving at home, sinking into a hot bath.

My bathrobe warming on the towel rail. Halogen glaring above.

Steam from the bath mingling with the centrally heated air of the bathroom.

No longer afflicted by a perilous fear of the toilet.

Never having to butcher a rabbit again.

Tumbling into my crisp clean sheets in my big warm bed, with the mattress firm and the pillows just the right sort of soft.

And I think of each day of pastel shades and shining kitchen appliances and the sense of nothing, nothing happening slowly and relentlessly, the diurnal round of bugger all, and I think of my husband leaving the house and me leaving the house and me returning to the house and my husband returning to the house and the irritating grind of our tyres on the newly paved drive and the click of our keys in the polished painted door and the formal salute as we sit down for our supermarket-sanctioned dinner and the smell of nothing, everything clean and unsmelling and the row upon row of similar houses with identical scenes spreading out around us, everyone in their identikit sanctioned lives.

I pause at the duck pond and look down into the dirt. Life grows in natural dirt, I think. Nothing grows in an ornamental pond. I'm contemplating this grand truth and then suddenly I think I'm not going back. It comes upon me suddenly and at first I don't accept it. I kick it back, hastily, worried the thought might grab me and make me do something I'll come to regret. But there it is again. I might not leave. Why should I, I think, just because my lazy traitor of a husband sent a postcard? Why should I leave at all?

That makes me panic. I get feverish trying to push back this treacherous little thought.

Here's your chance, some part of me is saying. *Get out while you can.*

I am standing there, somehow rooted to the spot. My brain pulsing, trying to shove this thought down below, as far down as I can get it, this evil coaxing thought, *Why not just stay?*

There is my diligent super ego going, *Get in the car, escape, today. She's expecting you to go.* And then somewhere else a voice of pure madness. *But I don't really want to go back.*

Yes you do, says my super ego. *You do want to go.*

And then the small Satan within. *Well, actually I'm not sure I do.*

I am beginning to realise — this thought has barrelled out of my unconscious and is now rattling around up there, in my frontal lobe, inescapable, really hammering on the walls and making a nuisance of itself — that I might actually stay.

BUT COME ON? But COME ON?

You are actually going to stay?

You are actually going to stay, in this mulch pit, with this madwoman and her bestiary of fetid beasts?

You are actually going to remain in the land of the thunderbox?

I am going to stay.

Preposterously, foolishly, illogically.

Despite my grand and abiding misery, despite the gelid mornings and the all-round sub-zero hell of my days I am going to stay.

I kick a pail across the yard. My God, I am going to stay. Lord Jesus, I am actually going to stay. I tear up the postcard and then I walk to the thunderbox and mmm the smell of matter, streaming into my lungs, and dearest I love you and — but I am ripping the card into tiny pieces and then I am — oh yet more horrible — hurling the pieces into the thunderbox.

I find I am laughing, and I wonder if this is my grand nadir or if there are further depths to plumb.

Can there be further depths?

I can't imagine but I know if there are then Cassandra will help me get right down to them. She will hand out the rope. Go on, further down. Yes, keep going. Oh you've reached the end of the rope? Well, just jump down. Yes, jump down, you're nearly at the bottom.

Really? Jump down? OK, if you're sure the bottom is so near

NEAAAAAAAAAAAAAAAAAAAAARRRRGH
Splat.

★ ★ ★

When I walk back into the kitchen, Cassandra says, 'Do you need any help putting your things in the car?'

And I say, sulkily, 'I'm not going.'

And she says, 'Well, then let's go and do the goats.'

It's impossible to tell if she's pleased or not.

If she cares at all.

We stride across the yard not saying anything and when we get to the goat pen there are no goats. The goats are not chewing their grass and butting the fence. They are not staring at me with their creepy malevolent eyes. They are not preparing to smash me into the mud.

There's a tear in the fencing and no goats.

I am just wondering whether this matters or not when Cassandra says, 'What have you done with the goats?'

'They're not there.'

'I can see that. Where are they?'

'I don't know.'

'Oh hell,' she says, and marches away.

I follow her, wondering if God has finally got bored with smacking me around and decided to smite her a bit. It seems the sort of thing a self-respecting deity really ought to do — you keep barking away and then eventually he decides it's time he zapped your goats. Kaaaapppppam, no more goats, how do you like that then? So I am thinking it is pretty pointless, if this is the case, to look for them but Cassandra is clearly not working on this theory. With a total lack of regard for the mysterious workings of the Lord she is stomping up the hill behind the house, shouting, 'Come out, you bastards. Descartes. Rousseau.

Where are you, you useless bastards?'

'Where have they gone?' I am running to catch up.

'Stupid bloody goats. They're determined to drag me into their foolish goat world.'

'Goat World,' I say. 'Now that's a place I'd like to go.'

Then I begin to laugh uncontrollably. This is doubtless an expression of the intense strain I am under and Cassandra looks at me in silence for a moment, but then she laughs too. We are hiking along the side of stream, where the neighbouring farmer's sheep are rustling in the bracken.

'Stupid bloody sheep,' I say, as we pass them.

'Nonsensical animals.'

Further up the hill is Beckfoot Cottage, which isn't a cottage at all, more like a mansion. There's an equally vast garden around it, full of flowers and blooms and apple trees bowing under their unpicked fruit, most of it pecked through or rotten. Today the garden also has the added presence of two goats. Busy ripping up the perfect borders, rearranging them nicely.

At the sight of them, Cassandra vaults over the gate.

'You barbaric ruminants, I'm going to kill you when I get hold of you. I'm going to put you in a fucking pot,' she roars, as she lands on the other side.

I follow her more slowly.

'Grab Descartes,' she says to me, gesticulating at the goat with an expensive row of flowers in her mouth. So I wander over to the goat and try to seize her by the collar. 'Hello, Descartes, nice Descartes,' I say, as she kicks me off.

'Come on, make more of an effort!' says Cassandra, who is by now holding Rousseau by a rope. 'Rousseau, you diabolical moron, come along with me. Why the hell can't you get hold of Descartes?'

'Because she doesn't want to come with me,' I say. 'She doesn't like me.'

'She doesn't like anyone. She's a goat.'

I make another lunge at Descartes and she blithely skips away.

'Bloody hell, hold this rope,' says Cassandra and races after Descartes. By now the goat is staring soulfully into the windows of the house. Cassandra gets hold of her, and, standing with the goat's rope in her hand, peers into the house as well.

'Just look at that,' she says.

I go over, dragging Rousseau behind me.

Before us: a beautiful sitting room, the sort of perfectly appointed place which makes my head pound with envy.

The fluid sculptural curves of expensive sofas.

A fireplace with slate surround and handsome wood mantel, a coffered ceiling and wide plank oak floors.

The whole place lavished with lucre.

The sort of luxury interior I once coveted, and which still has the power to make me stop and press my nose to the glass like a ravenous child left without pocket money outside a bun shop. Though I despise myself for it, I press my nose all the same.

'These people must be the biggest perverts of them all,' Cassandra is saying. 'They've owned this house for six years. I've walked past it every day, and only once have I ever seen anyone here. The guy bought it and decided he didn't like the rain. But he won't get rid of it, too good an investment, and he doesn't need to rent it out to make money because he's a banker. Ambrose Sooke he's called. Went to PoshSchoolOxbridge and then made a packet. That's what I heard anyway, I've never spoken to him.'

'He's really only been here once in six years?'

'They spent a year renovating it, filling the place with noise and builders. Hammer bang slap the granite kitchen and crash wallop the whirlpool in the bathroom and smash hammer the underfloor heating, and then they came to inspect it and lorded around the village for a couple of days and then they vanished forever.'

'What a waste of a whirlpool,' I say, thinking of it sitting there, with no one to whirl around in it.

'What a waste of a house,' says Cassandra. We stand there for a minute, me thinking about the whirlpool and the polished granite and Cassandra stony-faced and unusually silent.

Then, because the goats are stamping and complaining, we turn and lead them back down the lane. Beckfoot Mansion stands behind us, with the rising rain beating on its windows and no one to hear the storm.

9

I have blisters all over my hands, blisters which look as if I have the plague.

Each one is a bulbous cushion of pus, and some of them have sprouted parasite blisters, smaller bulbous pus cushions mounted attractively on the original pus pile.

When Cassandra sees them she neglects to offer any expression of sympathy or concern, but instead she grips my wrist and then she gets a big rusty needle and sticks it into each blister while I writhe in rage and agony and try to struggle free. But her hand is like a vice and I am clamped entirely.

When the needle goes into each blister yellow pus gushes out and I am left with my skin torn off and blood all over my hands.

By the time Cassandra releases me I am nearly weeping with fury and pain.

'Why in the name of Christ did you do that?'

'What?'

'What you just . . . did . . . to my hand . . . '

'You should always lance a blister.'

'That's a boil. You lance a boil. You should leave a blister alone, unless you're insane.'

'No no, blisters too. Never let a blister just sit there. The pus sac only slows you down.'

I am staring in disbelief at my hands and wanting vividly and acutely to punch her. I want to get her by the flame-hair and drag her into her garden, throw her into the thunderbox.

I allow myself a developed fantasy about forcing into her composting shit pit while screaming, 'THERE! That's natural goodness for you! LIKE IT? LIKE SOME MORE? WOULD YOU LIKE SOME MORE?'

But I am weak and a coward and anyway my hands are blazing with pain so I say, 'That's it. I'm going out. I'm going for a walk.'

★   ★   ★

Under a streaked storm-threatening sky I march down the lane. For a moment I'm not even interested in what Cassandra thinks. I am entirely indifferent to her system of reward and punishment. I don't care at all. I take my flayed hands and wash them in the river. The water is clouded white, like eggs beaten into peaks. My blood and pus mingle with the fresh water and the cold numbs my hands.

And here is the unsmiling farmer on his

90

mini-tractor, unsmiling as he approaches and unsmiling as he draws alongside me.

I stare irritably at his unsmiling face and he stares back and then he drives on.

A few things make me feel better. The chocolate and sandwiches I buy from the post office act as a sort of anaesthetic. It's the forbidden grain and sugar that enliven me. I get palpably and progressively happier as I shove chunks of sugar into my mouth, and when I've wallowed in this sin I start walking again.

Then I go to a pub and order a coffee. That makes me feel better too, sitting at a table somewhere that isn't White Farm, somewhere that doesn't smell of mould and damp and a dozen different sorts of manure. Instead the place smells of toilet cleaner and air freshener and pork pies. I breathe in deeply as if I am inhaling a rare and expensive perfume. *Eau de* Ginsters. *Parfait, mon cheri.*

At a corner table, I leaf through brochures. The Glass-Blowing Centre. The Dry Stone Wall Museum. The Aquarium and Wildlife Park. The walls are covered with the usual photographs of long-dead worthies holding a fish they've just hooked, or a brace of pheasants. A particularly long and lovely marrow. I imagine myself up there one day, memorialised for my brilliance in a vegetable patch. We marrow enthusiasts shall not see her like again, the caption will say. Now that girl knew how to harvest a turnip.

I plot my revenge, and that makes me feel better still.

Best served cold.

I'm simmering down and thinking about how I might be able to release her cow one night, how I could creep down and lead it off somewhere, or perhaps I could scatter lettuce-eating slugs across her vegetable patch, or entice a band of treacherous rabbits into the heart of the farm. I can think of a succession of evil deeds I would be happy to perpetrate, as long as the end result was Cassandra briefly felled, Cassandra shamed or at least thwarted.

I am trying to develop a plan but the people by the bar will keep bellowing. With each wild bellow I lose my train of thought and have to start again.

So one night I could add pepper to all her cider barrels.

So one night I could put glue around the top of the thunderbox. She likes it so much, she can stay there.

So one night I could . . . and then someone lifts up another bellow.

*   *   *

It turns out they're all up in arms about something, some local drama. Something terrible has happened, so terrible they have formed an anxious huddle by the bar. They're huddled up and waving their arms about. High-pitched in their indignation.

'They didn't.'

'I just don't believe it.'

'They never did.'

'I just don't understand.'

'Poor Mavis and Arthur Williams.'

'Never been any trouble to anyone,' they are saying. 'Always so kind and friendly. Always going out of their way to help you.'

* * *

And I'm thinking, perhaps I could poison her. Not fatally, just something which would send her cringing to the thunderbox, twenty times a day. An über-laxative, something really inconvenient and humiliating.

Or I could poison her dogs. Those stinking lurchers she loves so much. Surely I could murder a couple of lurchers.

* * *

Then I hear, 'Twenty-five years they've been there.'

'Is it really that long?'

'Oh yes, easily that long.'

'Why are they chucking them out?'

'It's the National Trust.'

'Greedy bastards.'

'They want to sell it?'

'You bet they do, prices as they are at the moment.'

'Greedy greedy bastards.'

The good villagers by the bar are downing pints in an outraged way, and then one of them starts saying how Old Esk Farm went for a clean million the other day and how Mortimer Grey made a killing.

'That cunning old southerner.'

'Hardly spent a day there, for a dozen years.'

'You never saw him in the village.'

'Well they won't get a million from Arthur and Mavis's house.'

'They'll get a fair packet.'

'A packet, that's true.'

'Greedy bastards.'

All their anxious talk is of the terrible plight of Mavis and Arthur Williams and now my plans for vengeance are interrupted by an image of this harmless old pair, who have been spending their days eating Mr Kipling's pies and doing crosswords, perhaps they have some grandchildren they like to give refined sugars to, and now they're packing up all their tins of boiled sweets and chocolate fancies and Mavis's house slippers and the contents of the cupboard under their stairs — a therapeutic rocking chair for Mavis's back, a sewing machine, a collection of walking sticks and Arthur's father's flying suit.

I imagine poor old Mavis and Arthur sitting on their suitcases waiting for some council van to come and pick them up, with the rubbish.

And one of the worthies is saying, 'There's all the holiday homes, empty most of the year, but they don't want to rent them to locals.'

'No you can't find anywhere in the country to rent.'

'But they've always lived in the valley. They'll be lost in Barrow.'

That's where the old go, when they get too depressing and smelly. When their houses are taken away from them and flogged, flogged on the bucking bronco market. To the highest bidder, flogged.

The old are sent into exile, to a merciless terrace by a main road.

With the juggernaughts passing in the night.

Rattling their cheap china.

And the sound of dogs from the house next door.

RATTLE RATTLE. BOW WOW BOW WOW.

That's the sort of measly end Mavis and Arthur will get.

Sleep blighted by the rattle of juggernauts over asphalt and the lecherous bark of a pack of hounds.

OFF YOU GO, to a blighted terrace.

OFF YOU GO, old man, with your rheumy eyes.

And you, old woman, smelling interminably of rose water.

I imagine Mavis and Arthur — uncertain, completely incapable of sorting things out for themselves — plain bewildered — and even in the depths of my rage I feel a sort of pity for them. To be unwanted. Old and unwanted. Cast out.

In the end they'll find themselves on some frightening housing estate where they don't dare to venture out after dark, and even in daylight Arthur will be violently mugged and forced to hand over the paltry amount of money in his pockets and after that he will decline rapidly and never be the same again. And both of them will be dead within the year.

★ ★ ★

When I get back to the farm I don't see Cassandra anywhere so I just go upstairs and shut the ragged curtains and fall into a swoon. I sleep deeply and when I wake I don't know where I am.

For a moment I think I might be in my house, that I've just slept with the windows open and the place has been filled with cold air. I think I must get to work. I must be late. I am just thinking how I have to get up and get to the office when I see the ugly pile of china on the dresser in the corner and I remember.

I am not at home.

I am nowhere near my home.

In a sense my home no longer exists.

Cassandra is in the garden, doing something to a pile of spinach. Her overalls are smeared with grime. Her hair looks particularly red and crazy and when I tell her about Mavis and Arthur she stands there clutching her head and brewing up a really torrid fit. She's like an ancient geyser, bubbling away, making all sorts of ominous noises, and then finally spewing out a boiling plume.

'The National Trust can rot in hell,' she says. 'I hope they're all wiped out by something really vile. Smallpox, I hope they all get fucking smallpox.'

Then she is silent for the rest of the day.

10

Cassandra is deep in thought. This is a spectacle. A labour.

The sun rises and beams down upon us and the day is calm and still, a thin mist falling across the highest mountains.

For hours we work and time skids along and when dusk falls I am bent into a knot from the gardening, and I have weeded a great line of soil, purged it entirely.

Then I milk the rancid lactating beasts and bring the warm milk in.

And Cassandra says nothing at all.

★   ★   ★

It's the following afternoon before she issues a statement.

She says, 'Perhaps we can kill Banker Sooke and give his house to Mavis and Arthur. We could just kill him, no one would mind. Next time he's here, we'll just go up there with the bloody blunderbuss and smear his guts across his sofa.'

'I think someone would mind.'

'Hardly. Mrs Banker Sooke, well she gets

the dough, she's a posh witch, I bet, I bet she's just a really greedy witch, so she doesn't actually care about anything except the dough. And Banker Sooke's had such a succession of slutty mistresses anyway, Mrs Banker Sooke stopped loving him years ago, after slutty mistress number forty-three, if she ever did. She probably has a phalanx of lovers too, servicing her boredom. And the little Banker Sookes will be all right. They get the dough and anyway they never see their father so they won't really miss him either. They've been at boarding school since they were four, so what do they care? Mrs Banker Sooke will phone them in the dorm. 'Just thought I should let you know, Pater has just gorn and been shot by a crazed maniac with a blunderbuss.' 'Oh, Mater, how awwwfully silly of him.' 'Hummmm, yar.' 'Well, Mater, must go, it's Binky Pinky's birthday and there's old jam boot for supper. Can you ask nursie to send more tuck thanks aawwwfully Mater. Toodle pip.' 'Toodle pip darling.' '

'Really, the aspersions you cast on poor Mr Sooke and his family.'

'Defend them all you like, I'm still going to blow him away.'

'If the little abandoned Sookes don't cause

you to hesitate then at least think of the white carpet.'

'We can clean the carpet. When we have killed Sooke and taken his house we will give it a good lathering.'

'I don't think violent murder will get you the house. Mrs Sooke will just sell it. She probably hates it. She'll flog it to Banker Sooke mark two and then you'll have to kill him too.'

'I hadn't thought of that,' says Cassandra.

She is silent for a moment.

'Well, perhaps you're right. Perhaps murdering him wouldn't actually help Mavis and Arthur. If it's of no immediate use then there seems little point doing it.'

'OK, if you say so,' I say.

Then Cassandra gives me a rabbit and with gritted teeth and my eyes half-shut I go whack whack whack whack whack and then I throw it into the pot.

She comes in when I've finished and stands behind me. I am waiting for some acknowledgement of the great progress I have made.

She says, 'Oh, my God, how dweadful. You've chopped off its little bunny wunny wabbit head.'

★ ★ ★

The next day Cassandra is mute once more, and this echoing eerie silence persists as we stack wood in the woodshed and collect eggs and I have to drag the goats around on their tethers for what seems an eternity while the rain lashes my face and hands.

Civilisations decline and fall and then rise again from the ashes while I drag the goats around in the hissing steaming rain.

Man evolves into a super being and then blows himself into smithereens and I am still standing in a pile of mud saying, 'Come here little goatlet, you little bastard goatlet. Come here my bastard goatlet.'

And finally after six trillion years of goat-dragging Cassandra turns up and stands by the fence, and she shouts across to me, 'Surely there must be some law. Something we can invoke. Like, if you don't use your big house for more than three years then you forfeit your right to it. It becomes common property. Something like that.'

'No, there's no such law.'

'Are you sure?'

'Yes, perfectly sure. Can you give me a hand with this goat?'

'Why isn't there? It's outrageous there isn't a law like that.'

'Well, that's the deal with private property.

You're a private individual with your private money. You buy your private property and you can do whatever you want with it. Because it's yours. Anyway, can you help me drag this goat?'

'No, you need the practice. What about times of emergency? In the Second World War, people who lived on their own in big houses had to take in lodgers. Evacuees, and so on.'

'Why's that relevant?'

'Mavis and Arthur are, to my mind, victims of another national crisis. The iniquity of wealth. The wildly unfair distribution of property, so the Sookes have loads of massive houses lying empty and the Williamses have nothing. That's surely a major calamity.'

'Unfortunately it's not regarded as a national emergency.'

'So we can't argue that Banker Sooke has a moral duty to share his house with other people?'

'No, we can't.'

'God, you're such a little gatekeeper,' she says. 'You're such a shitty little line-toer. No you can't. No you can't. Lah lah lah, you love it.'

'No, I'm just . . . '

'Lah lah lah lah lah,' she says. And she leaves me in the mud. In Goat World.

Ages pass. Deep is the silence.

In deepest darkest silence we unblock the rainwater irrigation system, or Cassandra does while I stand there in my wellingtons hoping that if I stay well back she won't bestow some disgusting task upon me.

We have tea in continued silence and after that we clean and hoe and mend and there is fencing to repair and some slops to throw over the side of the pig house, and the cow needs its straw changing, and the dirty straw has to be taken to the heap for manure, and the lactating beasts have to be drained of milk and the cow proffers its dugs with a friendly look in its eyes.

All the while we are unspeaking, like a pair of shabby old nuns, the last nuns in the nunnery, left to say nothing to each other until death wastes us.

As we finish dinner Cassandra says, 'What if we called Banker Sooke and asked if we could use his house? Simple, honest, surely not in any way illegal. Not murderous at all. I can get his number from Sally in the village. She has emergency numbers for all these second-home perverts.'

'Well, you can try. It's a total waste of time, but you can try.'

Then she lapses into thought again.

★　★　★

By Friday my faculties are so drained by the relentless crashing silence that I am merely grateful when Cassandra says, 'We have a plan.'

It's late afternoon and by then I've spent the day knee-high in slime and my face is glowing with wind-burn and the vestiges of sun.

And somehow my backache has acquired a new nagging dimension, as if my lower spine is disintegrating by the day.

My spine is hanging by a thread, and I am bent double with pain but I say, eagerly, 'Really? Did you speak to Banker Sooke?'

She's clutching a notebook and she has a strange look of glee about her. Her eyes are shining. 'Yes, I think Banker Sooke and I now understand each other very well,' she says.

When we go inside she puts the notebook on the kitchen table and opens it as if it is a precious ancient tome. On the first page she has written one word: RESETTLEMENT.

'Is that it?' I say.

'No, there's more.' And she turns the page.

Initial accommodation for resettlement:

Beckfoot Cottage — 6 bedrooms
— uninhabited for the past 6 years
Wolf Barn — roughly 12 bedrooms
— uninhabited for the past 15 years
The Old Vicarage — 5 bedrooms
— uninhabited
Riverbank — 4 bedrooms — uninhabited
Wilton Mill — 4 bedrooms — uninhabited. The grounds also contain 3 holiday
homes, also uninhabited except during
the Christmas holidays, meaning another
8 bedrooms
Longbridge House — 3 bedrooms — also
uninhabited except during Christmas

'What's this?' I say. 'What does it mean?'

'Mavis and Arthur Williams are in luck because Beckfoot Cottage has just become available.'

'You've persuaded Banker Sooke to rent it to them?'

'Unfortunately it turns out that Banker Sooke is a soulless pile of waste matter. It is with regret that I have decided we can no longer involve him in the process.'

'So he said no?'

'He never actually said no. He was extremely busy amassing his further millions.

He didn't have time to talk. Anyway, it's not important what he thinks.'

'But surely it's important what he thinks about you using his house?'

'No, it isn't. It was clear from our brief exchange that his entire world view is completely insane and it would be very dangerous if we were to pander to it.'

'So you're going to break into Beckfoot Cottage?'

'I don't like to use the term break in. It's a smutty emotive term. I will facilitate resettlement.'

'You're seriously proposing that you move people into this house? Like squatters?'

'I'm sick of walking past these empty houses. I've done it every day for years. It's time to do something.'

'I understand it's galling,' I say weakly. 'But what you're proposing is completely illegal . . .'

'These people are committing a terrible crime by never using these houses. I have devised a solution, whereby we can save them and others from the terrible consequences of their criminal behaviour.'

'You're aware that's not how the real law would see it?'

'I don't care.'

Say no, I think to myself.

Say no now and stop all of this.

So I say, 'I'm not going to have anything to do with it.'

'Oh, but you are,' says Cassandra very firmly. 'I need some help. Naturally you, like the resettlers, will be free of blame. Any trouble and I will explain that you thought I was in charge of renting these properties. No one gets punished apart from me; it's very simple. Anyway we need to get on with it. Paul Bowness is coming round tomorrow.'

'Who's he?'

'Our second candidate for resettlement. He will be resettled in Wolf Barn.'

There is a very small voice in my head, telling me this is the end and I really must leave.

This diminutive voice is eloquently explaining that I should tell Cassandra White that I really have to go, and then there is another voice — louder and less polite, beginning to boom with laughter and saying, 'What madness this is, what complete madness!'

11

'It could be worse,' Cassandra tells me. 'I could be proposing something much worse.'

What she is proposing is this:

There are eighteen houses in the immediate vicinity. One is Whistling Green Farm, where the Hodgsons have been for hundreds of years.

Then there are the other permanent residents — the Graveses in the white house over the river, the Haldanes who run the post office, old Mrs Askam in Duddon Cottage, Anthony and Jane Ellwood at Seatoller Grange, then Morris Byrne the retired shepherd and Paddy Arthurs in the almshouses.

Then there is James Meredith, the nature poet, who comes to his house at the weekends and spends the week in London. He walks up the mountains swinging a stick and agonising about whether you would say the sunshine looks like 'rods of gold' or 'strands of gold' and because of this, says Cassandra, we should simply ignore him as far as possible.

'And whatever you do, don't read his books,' she says.

'Why?' I say.

'Because they're a pack of lies.'

This means that ten houses are in the possession of the enemy, viz Banker Sooke and his ilk. ('Who will be referred to henceforth as the perverts,' says Cassandra.)

Five of the pervert dwellings are never used. Four are used about once a year. One is used from June to October and will therefore be left alone for the time being.

Pervert dwellings Beckfoot Cottage and Wolf Barn will be resettled immediately, as they have been empty for many years. Then there will be an adjustment period and then the next three pervert dwellings will be resettled.

Resettlement will proceed by word of mouth, to minimise the likelihood of news getting back to the perverts.

At a rough estimate there are forty pervert dwellings along the valley and of these thirty-two are almost never used. While we are resettling the first pervert dwellings, research will be conducted into the other pervert dwellings in the valley to verify frequency of use.

Pervert dwellings will be resettled in strict order: the never used, the very rarely used and — perhaps — the occasionally used. The old and infirm will only be settled in the never used.

The incontinent will only be settled in houses belonging to stockbrokers.

Resettlers will be told that an agreement has been made with the owner of the cottage, that they can live rent free while the pervert is not there.

Resettlers will be kept innocent of the real nature of their resettlement so they can't be prosecuted or blamed by the perverts.

Resettlers will only be local people who cannot find accommodation in the valley.

Épater les perverts . . .

I say, 'Well I can't imagine much worse.'

'I can,' she says.

★ ★ ★

That night Cassandra goes round to Beckfoot Cottage to make the necessary arrangements, as she calls them with a sudden talent for euphemism.

She goes with a brick and a wrench.

And I follow her, protesting all the way.

Don't do this.

You really don't have to do this.

I don't think you should do this.

At the low stones I say, 'No,' and as we pass the Quaker burial ground I say, 'No,' and under the big yew tree I say, 'No'. Then the cock crows and suddenly I am Peter, is that

110

right? But there's no cock crowing anyway and besides Cassandra just ignores me and keeps walking up the hill and I keep stumbling along behind her nonetheless.

Despite my efforts in naysaying I am still there behind her. Tagging along.

When we arrive Cassandra smashes a downstairs window with the brick and clears the glass away with the wrench. The shattering glass really rings around the valley and I hear a dog barking somewhere. We're quiet for a few minutes, and then Cassandra goes in.

I stay outside. I am the coward trembling by the gate. There's a full moon and it's so bright you can see every blade of grass. There's a high wind and the night is full of ominous noises, creaks and clatters that make me want to turn and run.

Then Cassandra comes out through the front door.

'We're in luck,' she says. She's holding a set of keys.

'If I have this aright, then these . . . ' — and yes, the keys open the door.

'Perfect,' she says. 'Come on in.'

'I'm not going in there,' I say.

'Don't be ridiculous,' she says. 'Of course you are. Why else have you come?'

We go inside, wiping our boots. The place

smells of expensive antique furniture and expensive contemporary building materials.

'Chemicals,' says Cassandra, screwing up her nose.

We pass into the living room, where soaring windows frame the bucolic view — dark now, but by day there must be a perfect vista of mountains and trees — and the polished oak floor creaks beneath our crass feet.

There is the custom cast-stone fireplace I so admired from the garden.

And beside me is a Regency period chaise longue in finest rosewood, with scrolled arms, moulded legs.

Set at rakish angles, a delicious set of Regency period mahogany cane armchairs, with lotus-carved tapering front legs.

A sofa table with lion's paw castors.

The place looks rich as anything. Not for the Sookes the mass-produced fripperies of modern furnishing. They will have their £50,000 table and they will place upon it a copy of the 1998 *Deer Hunter's Almanac*, as if there is the faintest hope in hell of Banker Sooke going off to slay a beast.

In the kitchen there are granite counters, a wall oven, a sub-zero refrigerator.

The sort of dishwasher that cleanses all your finest china without a sound. Without a scratch. An automated scullery maid.

A cast-iron wood burner.

I can hardly comprehend it all. My heart is dancing and thumping in my breast. The most scared I've been . . . the most scared . . . the most exhilarated, perhaps . . .

Upstairs — up the sweet-smelling oak stairs and along the landing.

There is a statue of a man carrying a flagon of wine, supported on a plinth.

On the walls embroidered pictures, done up in silk and satin. Every bedroom with sheets on the beds, towels neatly laid out.

Everything is aligned geometrically, every picture is rail straight and every towel forms a perfect rectangle on the bed. Naturally it beats my lost suburban idyll into a pulp. It makes me look just the sort of duped slave I truly am, trotting off to the OKA sale and filling up my car. Lying on my Japanese-style bed, along with half a million others. Lying there and imagining I was the apogee of style.

Here is style, say the Sookes, but casually, because they don't care what we think anyway.

In one bedroom there's an eighteenth-century knee-hole dressing chest.

In one bathroom a Chippendale-period gilt-wood mirror. Naturally just the thing for the bathroom, and a mere £20,000.

Then, lest we think the Sookes are stuffy

113

antique freaks, there's the gleaming new bathroom with the whirlpool at the centre. So inviting I think, standing over it, assessing its smooth untouched sides with a covetous eye — just a quick whirl, a brief whirl-about — but Cassandra is saying, 'OK, you've ogled it all enough.'

But but — I want to say — I've hardly begun to appreciate the fineries, the fripperies, the gentle combination of elegance and frivolity, the dainty architectural jokes, the frissonic mingling of aesthetic styles, the beauty and the comedy, the radiance of unsullied unlived-in perfect homeliness.

I've nearly regressed to my earlier state. Any slight progress of recent weeks, any nascent appreciation of the simple life — simple life be damned, I'm thinking.

I want a whirlpool and a tallboy and a linen press.

I want a chiffonier and as soon as I work out quite what one is I am damn well going to buy one. Or dream of buying one . . .

I want a satinwood card table.

I want their row upon row of leather-clad books.

I want a matching pair of celestial and terrestrial globes by G. and J. Cary of St James's Street London, whoever the hell they are.

And in the wine cellar below I think that I don't know the first thing about wine but I imagine a Chateau Filhot 1937 can hardly come cheap. I can't see myself picking it up on special offer from the supermarket.

But now I lift my head from devout contemplation of a brass-bound oval wine cooler and Cassandra is looking at me in disgust.

'You're pathetic,' she says.

'I'm just astounded by how much money they've spent on stuff they've never used. Outrageous,' I say. 'Scandalous. Truly appalling.'

'Rubbish,' she says. 'You should be ashamed of yourself. This place is a freak show.'

'It's not so bad.'

'It's grotesque. These people are nuts. They think this is the country style. But it's a parody from start to finish. The countryside is just a fantasy for people like this, a place where you roam through the so-called scenery by day, allowing the elements occasionally to ruffle the folds of your expensive outdoor wear, where you can always retreat to your roaring fire, your pristine house. If you have become tainted in any way by earth, mud, the materials of the countryside, you run off to your whirlpool

— urgh, dirt — and cleanse yourself. And then you go to the kitchen for a hearty game casserole which you probably didn't even cook yourself, served on the oak table you ordered from London.'

'Sounds nice enough to me.'

'They think this is authentic country living because they are surrounded by wood and stone and natural fibres — even though they're not actually from the neighbourhood at all, even though everything in the house has travelled thousands of miles. They think this is real rustic bliss because they have *English Cooking* and *Game Recipes* in their stack of unused cookery books in their unused kitchen, and because there is an unused Aga in the corner and a view of hills through the window. It's all just a crazy dream they're having, and because they never test it for more than a few days a year, they never have to snap out of it. They think they love the countryside. But really they are the death of the countryside, the scourge of it.'

'Isn't that a bit ungrateful when you're about to commandeer their house?'

'I am doing them a favour.'

'I don't think they'd agree.'

'I am saving their souls.' She pauses.

Then, 'I am saving their shitty stinking souls.'

12

Beckfoot Cottage has been resettled.

The handover was strange enough. Two bent-backed pensioners deluging Cassandra with thanks. Clutching little suitcases as they walked, like refugees. Tottering along on bucked and bandy legs.

Mr Williams said, 'We're so grateful. We've been worried sick,' and Cassandra shrugged and said, 'It's what the owners should do. Morally it's the right thing. They never use it,' and the Williamses said, 'Oooh, but I remember this house, didn't the Arkwrights live here for years, old John Arkwright died and his son went away, left for foreign parts, and so he just sold the house, that's right, the Arkwrights they had a lovely garden back here,' and then the grand opening of the door, the revelation of the unmitigated wealth of the interior, the marble and granite and slate and all the whole hoard of antique furniture looking so smooth and polished and smelling so sweetly, and the Williamses were stunned and silent for a moment, still holding their little suitcases and not knowing where to turn.

A heady sense of unreality, as we stood in the living room admiring the view from the French windows. The upper valley ablaze in afternoon sunshine.

Mrs Williams set her ugly suitcase down by a revolving drum table, nearly bowing to it as she did, and said — the sun shining on her ravaged face — 'Oooh it's so lovely are you sure are you sure?' and Cassandra — magnanimously and as if the place was in her power to give or withhold, which in a sense it was, but only because she was the arch thief of it all — replied, 'I'm so glad you like it. Make yourselves at home.'

Cassandra had produced a little brochure. Somehow she had typed it up and even driven into the grey town to print up some copies. There was a copy on the card table, as if left there by a cleaner or virtuous employee of the 'Valley Resettlement Scheme'.

'Dear Resettler,' it said. 'We do hope you'll enjoy your stay in our accommodation. There are some basic house rules which our coordinator will explain to you. Other than that, please feel free to enjoy the valley.'

It did not say, 'Dear Resettler, If a really angry pervert turns up and demands to know who the hell you are, don't panic. They are clearly experiencing some pervert delusion that you have broken into their house. Just explain to them quietly that they are not feeling well. Then tell them calmly but firmly to go away.'

★ ★ ★

A heady sense of madness lurking, and the threat all the time of being caught.

The troubling spectre of Banker Sooke.

Banker Sooke was among us, in his severely expensive artworks, and his leatherbound library, and his mahogany double serpentine desk, where he had even left a laptop. Not the most up-to-date model because of course he hadn't been here for six years. But there was a computer nonetheless, all rigged up with broadband and with an impregnable password which we couldn't crack. (Though we typed in Banker. Gold. Lucrelovelylucre. Satanismyfriend.)

Banker Sooke made a few appearances in framed photographs, at least I assumed it was him — tall and dark-haired, perhaps a little jowly in his over-fed midlife, but nothing too grave, nothing he couldn't smuggle into a well-cut suit, and as we passed I asked him to forgive us.

He didn't look like the sort of guy who would.

And the poor old Williamses — unaware of

what was really going on, unaware of everything except the glittering spoils of the place and the room after room of bureaux and settees and davenports and gilt and green leather — were speechless with awe, a bedraggled man with a faceful of swollen veins and an old woman with swollen ankles, both of them long past their primes. Those primes vanished during the last world war, and they looked like worn-out blown-down husks, human lean-tos smashed up by years of storms. They dragged their rickety bones upstairs, and we dragged their bags, and by the time we got to the third bedroom Mrs Williams was nearly crying.

'I've never seen such a beautiful house,' she said. 'It's like a palace.'

I thought of her wiping her gnarly old hands on the deep comfort Egyptian cotton towel set.

Setting out her cheap perfumes on the George II caddy top chest.

Washing her few last strands of hair under the whisper-quiet power shower.

Lowering her wasted limbs into the whirlpool.

She looked like she would be whirled away, she was so wispy and skinny. A sudden end for Mrs Williams, whirled down a super deluxe Jacuzzi. They would say, well at least she died happy. Doing what she loved.

Whirling.

'If you use this bedroom, that would be best,' said Cassandra, taking them to the plush master bedroom complete with magisterial bed and overmantel mirror.

They stood there, staring around. It was hard to tell what they were feeling. They were so hunched and bowed down anyway, and then there was the weight of their confusion.

'I'll bring the rest of your things over later,' said Cassandra. She explained the rules to them. Briskly. And she said she would bring them some wood. Mrs Williams sat down on the bed, on the silk bed throw. She touched it with her hand. 'I just never knew people had houses like this,' she said.

'Just ask me if you don't understand how something works,' said Cassandra. 'They have loads of gadgets — stereos, fancy TVs, and so on, so let me know if you can't do them.'

They'll never work them, I thought. They've been slapping the back of a flickering fifties TV set for the last few decades, coaxing it into revealing a few snowstorm scenes. They'll be sitting there for a month with a multi-channel remote control in their hands, not knowing what to point it at.

* * *

'Don't you think it's a bit of a waste?' I said to Cassandra as we walked home.

'What do you mean?'

'Well, they'll just settle in and then they'll be really happy and then they'll get thrown out in a few weeks' time when the owner realises what you've done.'

'Perhaps they won't get thrown out. Perhaps they'll die there.'

'Only if Sooke comes back and shoots them.'

'At least then they won't have to find anywhere else to live.'

'This idea is full of holes. It is nothing but holes.'

'Don't fix on the minutiae. Just stand back and admire the grandeur of the overall scheme.'

And she patted me on the back. 'I would never have thought of it without you,' she said.

Smiling like a happy ogress.

13

Today there's a boy downstairs. He's burly and handsome. His is not a subtle sort of beauty, it's a broad, hard, lithe-bodied late-twenties sort. It's unabashed and flashy. He has abundant fair hair and a wind-blown face and large capable hands and it's impossible to imagine he will grow old.

Most likely he'll look like this for years anyway.

I'm standing there admiring this boy when Cassandra says, 'This is Paul Bowness,' and I realise he isn't just an apparition I conjured on which to slake my sexual frustration, but rather a flesh-and-blood candidate for resettlement.

He is actually here, and so am I it seems and Cassandra is even introducing me as her assistant, which irritates me but I don't say so, and Paul is nodding towards me.

I say something inaudible back to him, at least I hope it's inaudible because I don't think it's much more than, 'He.'

Cassandra says, 'She will show you where you'll be resettled.'

'It's a funny name you've given this,' says Paul.

'Why do you think it's funny?' says Cassandra.

'I can't imagine how it happened.'

'It's a simple understanding we've reached with the owners,' says Cassandra.

'I don't really see what they get out of it.'

'They get the joy of seeing others made happy,' says Cassandra breezily. 'Also it means we hate them just a little less.'

'They hardly ever come here. I wonder why they care,' says Paul.

He's terse and direct, and you have the sense it would be hard for him to lie. Hardly the best addition to the scheme, I think. Asks questions, natively honest.

Preposterously handsome.

All in all, a certain disaster.

'The owners have amassed a sizeable karmic debt. I'm helping them to pay it off. If they don't thank me on this turn of the wheel, they may well do on the next,' says Cassandra.

'I simply don't know what you're talking about,' says Paul, smiling and shaking his head. He turns to me, 'Do you understand anything Cassandra says to you?'

'Ne,' I say.

'This will help,' says Cassandra, handing

him one of her typed-up pamphlets. 'Now my assistant will walk you to Wolf Barn. I have to get down to something in the garden.'

I can't really protest, even though my natural instinct is to flee.

★　★　★

It's unwieldy. Cassandra's scheme is unwieldy enough, and now I'm struggling with another affliction. It's unwieldy as we step through the mudslide at the bottom of the drive and walk under the pelting rain. It's plain unwieldy as Paul says, 'So, how did Cassandra really persuade those rich people to rent out their places?' and I say, 'Oh, I don't really know.'

Wolf Barn is deep in the woods, at the end of the bridle path. So that's a fine unwieldy walk, as Paul says, 'So how did you even find the Swiss people to ask them? I've never seen them in the valley.'

Incoherent, drunk on a heady cocktail of nerves and self-recrimination, I try to fob him off with some drivelling nonsense about Cassandra having phoned every Herschman in Switzerland until she found the right one. He nods slowly but I don't think he's convinced.

'Naturally it makes sense to let someone

125

else live there for a while,' I say hopefully.

'Does it?'

We endure a spell of silence, which becomes progressively more awkward and unwieldy in its own way, though in one sense it's preferable to the questions I can't answer and the sound of my nerves.

It's a relief when we arrive at Wolf Barn because that stops the unwieldiness of our walk, though no sooner have I breathed more easily than I am wrestling with a new variety of unwieldiness. A lying my head off variety. A fearful and guilty variety, as if we may be apprehended any moment. An IS THIS ALL A DREAM? and AM I REALLY SOMEWHERE ELSE? total neurotic collapse variety.

Fortunately there's plenty to see. Wolf Barn is a mini village. It's an entire slate schloss, with a low wall around it. The houses are arranged around a courtyard, and beyond that are some unused fields gone to brambles.

I jangle the keys thinking how unwieldy and how did this happen, how did I end up in this unwieldy mess, standing here about to lodge someone illegally in a rustic pile?

It's certainly not what I was envisaging when I came to the countryside.

My hand trembles when I turn the key in the door because I suddenly think I hear a noise inside.

'Steady,' Paul says, and I see he's noticed my nerves. 'Don't get too excited.'

In return I laugh in a shrill squawking way, twitch and mutter and generally do a convincing impersonation of a lunatic on day release.

The place is vast. It's vaulted like a cathedral, with great oak beams high above us and light streaming in from arched Gothic windows. The whole place is shining in the sunlight; the dust is shining, clouds of it floating upwards, flying dirt glinting like diamonds.

We stand in the engulfing clouds of dust and we cough together, and Paul says, 'Christ Almighty. It's completely abandoned.'

At the heart of the first room is a long oak table. The table goes on and on in one direction and on and on in the other. You could have your own mead hall in here, your own suite of thanes clutching flagons of ale.

Beyond the table is a living room, gigantic sofas still dwarfed by all the space, a gargantuan dusty television. Then there's a kitchen fitted out in slate and wood with massive windows revealing the fields in their stripped-down beauty.

For all the sumptuous vastness there's a dusty smell to the place, a musty old neglected smell. There's the flying dust and the furniture is clad in sheets. When we start lifting them off, we release fifteen years of settled dust layers. With each tug, five billion particles of ancient grime lift off, sally forth towards the roof.

Lift off! And there's a big black leather armchair, brand new, the leather stiff and crackling.

Dust particles lift off! And there's a coffee table, all in glass and chrome. Then, another ten million dust particles later, an entire grand piano, all out of tune.

Then a Wurlitzer.

In another room the dust clouds part to reveal a ping-pong table and a punch bag.

In another, a writing table with bandy legs. And inside there are piles of crested writing paper.

Herr Robert Herschman
Wolf Barn
Duddon Valley
Cumbria

King of the Dust Clouds.
Absent Lord of the mead hall.
Let us lift a flagon to Herr Herschman in his perpetual absence.
'That was the father,' I say, as if we are in a museum. As if I am the curator and reigning

128

expert on the life and times of Herr Herschman and his empire of dust. 'The son is called something else. Johann, the son is called.'

'Really,' says Paul.

And upstairs through the dust smog we discern: a dressing table, a series of sumptuous bedrooms, a pile of sombre landscape paintings, a few dozen standard lamps, and, finally, a bedroom with a four-poster bed.

'They really haven't been here for years, have they?' says Paul.

'No. The son has never used the place at all. After the father died, everyone thought he would at least come and inspect it. But he didn't even want to see it.'

'But it's so plush,' he says. 'There's so much stuff in it.'

'It's strange he didn't want to take a look.'

'I've been living in my dad's garage for two years. We converted it into a bedroom. I had a TV and a fridge, but the place always stank of oil.'

'Did you move out the car?'

He laughs. 'Of course I did. What did you think I was doing, sleeping on the bonnet every night?'

'Sounds as if you were.'

'Anyway this is ridiculously fancy.'

'Once it's had an airing, I think it will be quite adequate.'

Paul has been working as a part-time sheep shearer, he tells me. Sometimes he paints houses. 'I'll do anything,' he says. 'I'm practical. Good with my hands.'

And oh my optimistic spirit. There he is, unlined and vivid with youth and me just another cast off proto-spinster, but I'm thinking there's a sort of ambiguity to his voice, as if he's offering an innuendo, though a second later I have dismissed it as a phantom generated by my ravenous hyperactive imagination. The base cravings of my body, causing auditory hallucinations. Eventually I will become so tragic and alone that reality will shimmer distantly behind the consoling edifice of my fantasies.

Yet now I'm saying, in an effort to sound efficient, 'So, we'd like to move others in gradually. We'd like the outhouses occupied, and eventually we'll use the fields for cattle and vegetables. And we thought you might like to bore for water, then the house will be self-sufficient in that respect.'

So that when old Herr Herschman comes back he can go really ballistic.

Paul nods. 'Fine,' he says. 'I don't mind.'

We've been wandering around for ages already but there are still three outhouses to investigate, filled themselves with concealed treasures. There too, we find everything is grandiose, every table is made to seat a rowdy retinue and every bed is twice king-sized. Emperor-sized. Lord of the universe-sized. Every bed is its own country of sheets, a continent of duvets.

It's like tiptoeing into a giant's palace, as if any moment a great fist will snatch us up and there'll be a deafening roar.

Fee fi fo fum.

It's almost wearying, these successive lofty ceilings, cavernous fireplaces, kitchens with their walk-in fridges and lay-down-your-quarry tables. And then there are the flying configurations of dust, like a disassembled ghost.

Gusting at us as we walk around. Infiltrating our lungs.

I throw open window after window and still the place is riddled with these mournful drifting dust ghosts. Spectres of former intruders, left to wander the giant's lair.

Fee fi fo fum.

Perhaps the fist won't even pick us up, I think. It'll just come down on our heads.

BAM, splat.

★　★　★

In the courtyard we stand looking up at the big blank windows. The river is full, gushing past the end of the garden.

'Well there's certainly plenty of room,' says Paul. 'I can think of a few mates who'd leap at the chance to live here.'

'You could let them know there's space if you like.'

'OK.'

'They can help with the crops and cattle,' I say.

'Cassandra really must be a good talker,' he says. 'I always knew she could really bang on but I never thought she'd manage to persuade anyone. She's hardly diplomatic.'

'How long have you known her?'

'Oh, she married my cousin. But I knew her family before. They've been in the valley for donkey's years, as long as anyone can remember. She says there have been Whites in the valley since the sixteenth century.'

'So her husband took her name?'

'Yes, it was easier with the farm.'

'I'm very sorry about what happened to your cousin.'

'We all are. But no one took it harder than Cassandra.'

Silence enfolds us again. I stumble, try to think of a way to emerge from under it, but then he says, 'Why did you come here?'

'Oh, I answered an advert.'

'To work on this scheme?'

'No, to work in Cassandra's house. Helping with her smallholding.'

'How do you find it up here?'

'It was hard at first. Now . . . well . . . ' *At first I was confused, now I'm just washed along,* I think. *I drift with the tide.* 'Well, it gets easier.'

'What does? The work or living with Cassandra?' he says.

'Both.'

'In her heart she's a kind woman,' he says.

I pause to grapple with the strangeness of this remark; I wonder at it for a few minutes and still it sits there, impossible and indigestible, so I say, 'Well, I hope you find everything you need.'

He shrugs. 'It's all far too nice for me. If you insist on me staying here then I'll naturally try my best not to ruin it.'

'Good,' I say. 'I'll leave you to settle in. Let me know if there's anything you need. Here's your key.'

'Thanks,' he says. He takes the keys and I think he might be about to shake my hand. But he doesn't. My hand stays there for a brief instant, and I feel my cheeks flaming like a schoolgirl.

'See you soon,' I say.

* * *

MADNESS, MADNESS — I am shaking my head as I crash back through the wood, sliding on the slippery stones, jumping over flooded streams. Pure madness. I have been in a fog, perhaps exhaustion, or nascent hypothermia, or the brain-softening effects of quinoa, anyway my reason has been stunned and now I am clinging to my fleeting awareness of How Things Really Are, not how I would like them to be or — Still Worse — how Cassandra would like them to be. Clearly anyone who allows Cassandra's notion of how things should be to in any way define her experience of reality is doomed, DOOMED utterly, and I realise with a spasm of horror that I have slipped into this crazy state, this abnegation of sense and dereliction of . . . OF . . .

Fee fi fo fum

The thought is fading and I try to cling to it. The sense of madness is fading even as I run through the wood. It's a will-o'-the-wisp moment of clarity, receding as I pursue it.

Receding as I stop on the path and try to grasp it again.

Not so bad at present, I think, only three people to explain things to. Someone — i.e. me, because there isn't a hope of it being

Cassandra — must be calm, measured, reasonable.

Be she alive or be she dead.

I'll grind her bones to make my bread.

Someone must be reasonable, I think, and now I run back to the farm holding this single phrase in my brain. Someone must be reasonable, and when I get there flushed and panting I explain to Cassandra — calmly, eloquently — that her scheme is too risky, that she should stop now, that Paul and the Williamses should be moved out as soon as possible.

'There is no way this can work. You will certainly be caught and you will lose everything.'

Cassandra thinks for a minute, then says, 'Who cares?'

Then she goes back to making cheese.

★ ★ ★

This is, I am beginning to realise, the central difference between Cassandra and me.

Cassandra has lost everything already.

She is liberated from desire.

She is really in a Zen state.

A Buddhist might even admire her. In her next life she will most likely not return as a monkey or an ant. God knows quite what she will return as, but it won't be as bad as my next turn on the wheel.

Cassandra craves no earthly luxuries or comforts and she is prepared to work herself to death.

She is indifferent to human authorities and ignores the nagging demands of the flesh, whereas I am not and cannot.

I am not indifferent at all and am rather entirely controlled by these authorities and demands.

I am most likely to return in the next life as a slug or a tree frog.

There's no redemption for someone as steeped in desires as me.

14

So now we're waiting.

The burglary has begun and we are waiting for someone to notice. We're waiting for Banker Sooke to return, or for an enraged Swiss man to emerge from the forest.

We're waiting for the knock on the door, the ferocious accusation, the resounding cry of 'What the hell have you done to my house?'

We're waiting for that lazy old divinity to finally pummel us or for the law to condemn us.

It is perplexing but it seems that if you discreetly break into a couple of neglected second homes and install some permanent residents, no one actually cares. Perhaps a few locals have their suspicions but they keep quiet.

The old farmer still refuses to acknowledge me and putters past as if I am invisible, and the rest still nod grimly when I pass.

No one mentions anything to Cassandra, as far as I can see.

She's busy anyway, preparing the next stage of the scheme, drawing up a list of people who will join Paul in Wolf Barn, organising residents for Riverbank, the Old Vicarage, Wilton Mill and Longbridge House.

★ ★ ★

The next time I go over to Wolf Barn I am bringing a little consortium of prospective residents — young families and a few friends of Paul's, all of them grateful and nervous and tragically oblivious to the criminal nature of their occupancy, crunching behind me through the wood like a tour group, and me jangling the keys and trying to look nonchalant.

Welcome, I say, grandly.

Welcome to the dust palace.

The giant's castle.

In the forest Wolf Barn is less abandoned than before.

Outside the door is a mountain bike. And inside there's a smell of wood and perhaps a background trace of PG tips. A cup and saucer at one end of the mead table, looking small and out of place. In the kitchen there are the remains of Paul's efforts at cooking, a pan with some old stew in it and a can of soup. The walk-in fridge has a bottle of milk in it and a bag of sausages.

In all this immensity I can't find Paul,

though I call for him. I call in an urgent eager voice, but there's no reply. My heart stops pounding and my hands stop sweating and my body becomes still with disappointment.

A hiatus.

People are milling around, gazing up at the monumental ceilings and the light gushing through the windows and one of them is fingering the piano in a nervous reverential way. There's a young couple — Nicola and Chris, who Cassandra has decided will be in charge of one of the outhouses, and Nicola says — holding a baby in her arms — 'Isn't it so grand? Isn't it beautiful? Aren't we lucky?'

You'd better hope you are, I think.

I hand out keys, tell them where to get their bedding, that we'll find some money to get them some animals. I suggest they draw up a rota.

'Get wood from the forest. Paul is going to organise a well,' I say.

'How long can we stay here?' someone asks, some over-curious man with sparse blond hair and jug ears.

'At present there is no time limit set,' I say.

'When will there be?' he says.

'Will there be what?'

'A time limit set?' He has a wispy wife with long black hair, and their toddler is tugging at their trousers, wanting to be picked up. Matty they keep calling him. Matty, don't do that. No, Matty, don't eat the dirt. Don't lick the stones. NO, Matty, NO!

'At present there's no time limit. I can only speak about the present situation,' I say.

Matty, give that to Mummy. Matty don't stand on the piano. Don't decapitate that worm with that spoon. Don't — OH GOD, Matty, NO!

They file off into their houses, partially grateful, partially suspicious, or somehow disbelieving. Perhaps they sense something is awry. Perhaps not. The thing is incongruous all the same. For years they've seen the place from the forest path — the big iron gates, forbidding drive, the colossal outlines of the barns.

'I walked past here every day as a child,' says one burly man with a permanent frown. 'I never thought I'd be living here.'

Well, the slate schloss is open, I think, as I scamper back along the forest path. The slate schloss is well and truly opened up, the doors have been kicked down and we have gone beyond the point of no return.

* * *

Lo, said someone or other, and thus it was that Cassandra White, who had been somewhat beyond the norm for a few years, not quite blazing in her strangeness but definitely flickering gently with it, decided that she would continue with her blatantly illegal scheme, and thus it was that Gladys and Robert Wadsworth, who had just discovered that their roof was falling down and lacked the money to repair it, were resettled in the echoing vastness of Longbridge House, there to rattle around their three bedrooms and watch 24-hour-a-day multi-channel TV, and thus it was that Matthew and Tabitha Yates, who had been asked by their landlord to move out because he had decided to sell up, were resettled in the Old Vicarage and couldn't believe what they found.

And thus too did Irene Gibbs of Great Gables Farm, who hadn't really been able to cope with the place since her husband died, but who had only ever rented from the National Trust and so couldn't afford to buy elsewhere, find herself the proud resettler of Riverbank. And thus did John Frank who had a dodgy leg find himself limping around the lovely corridors of Wilton Mill. And he was joined there in the guest houses by Sandy Heptonstall and his daughter Maria, and Roger and Louise Avery, who never had two pennies to rub together and were always moving from place to place, and Maureen Addlestone, whose husband had died a long while ago and who found the draughts and isolation in her slum cottage on Birker Fell had made her ill for successive winters.

And thus it was that I went down with each party to their designated accommodation and saw them nearly tearful as they went from one room to another — all of them marvelling and silent, not wanting to touch anything, moving slowly as if in a dream.

Uncertain where to turn, and hardly comprehending that they would sleep that night in the master bedroom and tousle the immaculate sheets.

I was the tour guide on our frankly peculiar tour — welcome to the lives of the rich, that for some reason you are going to experience gratis, in a one-off experiment you will Live Like the Rich for No Money at All!

Welcome to the house which will never get cold. Or damp. Or too hot. Or too dry. The house which is regulated for maximum comfort. All sorts of little switches and valves are working inconspicuously away to ensure you are permanently comfortable. You will never shiver or sweat again.

And welcome to the kitchen, which is full of gleaming shining things.

And welcome to the serried rooms,

impossibly constant in their beauty.

And here we have an ornament of great elegance and age.

And here we have a portrait of the owner's mother, who was clearly also rich, wealth bubbling in her veins, wealth as her origin and destiny.

And here is the bathroom, which is full of heat and light, heat and light are the twin forces of this house, all of them staving off cold and darkness which are evils and must therefore be banished.

And here is a bookcase full of contemporary accounts of global finance and the economic crisis that is upon us and classic novels and picture books from gaudy exotic places and a lot of Graham Greene and Hardy and Austen and Dickens — holiday reading for the owners, who are as clever as they are rich, nothing too arduous as they kick back and forget their high-achieving ordinary lives, but nothing too flimsy either.

Here they are on retreat, expecting pleasure.

And here we have the accoutrements of pervert pleasure — the multi-channel TVs and board games and DVDs in neat rows and CDs precisely ordered on their CD stack and the iPods and MP3 players and the children's playroom with its tasteful wooden train set and doll's house, the sort of doll's house you would actually rather like to live in, were you proportioned in the right way, and pleasure echoes from the ceilings and ricochets around the white-washed gleaming walls.

'Here you will find everything you need,' I say to my astounded clients.

They are speechless.

They are open-mouthed and staring.

'Can we really live here?' they stutter. 'It is true?'

'Oh yes,' I say.

But Lo, of course it isn't true, and therein lies the biggest problem.

'We do hope you enjoy your stay,' I say to them all.

Somehow it's always me, showing them around. I am the smirking flunky, a housekeeper of stolen houses, jangling the keys. A semi-reformed pervert myself, still salivating at the sight of a really lovely pelmet. When we convert a house — requisition, steal, however you're phrasing it — after the initial break in — Cassandra with a wrench, a discreet tinkle of glass — we hope to find a spare set of keys. If we can't find a spare set of keys we change the locks. Ingenious, and gives you another few minutes when the owners finally turn up. Jangling the keys, I march the resettlers into their new homes and

I stroke the fine carpets and breathe in the smell of polished pine and then I receive thanks. I receive torrents of thanks, because these resettlers have never seen such fine pervert palaces before.

'It's so kind of you,' they say, while I raise my arms and make noises like 'Pish, pish'.

'You must come round for dinner,' they say, and I say, 'Yes, that would be great, thanks,' all the while thinking, 'But perhaps I won't . . . Perhaps I won't sit with you waiting for the perverts to return . . . '

But I say, 'Well, see you soon,' and then I hand over the keys and vamoose. I scram, my heart pounding, and I always get a head rush when I get out, and realise I haven't yet been caught.

This must be why people turn to crime. Their lives are dull and harsh and they do the same dull thing every day and someone tells them they will have to do it forever. Just to make nothing. Just to subsist.

And then they see wealth and they don't have it. They don't have it and they'll never get it. And they see the disregard the wealthy have for their wealth, the way they take it for granted. It's clear the perverts don't really give a damn about their houses. It was easy enough for them to clad them in finery, drape them in silks and linens and portraits of

Uncle George, but after that they lost interest. The houses are immaculately tidy because the perverts pay a local woman to clean. They are equipped with everything because furniture and gadgets cost very little, if you're a super-wealthy pervert.

I begin to see how these over-equipped abandoned houses have ground away at Cassandra for years and finally goaded her into action.

Later, always later, I tell Cassandra how it's not going to work.

'Are you hoping for squatters' rights?' I say. 'So when the owners come back you refuse to budge?'

'We can't lose,' says Cassandra. 'If they don't come back, we get lots of accommodation for these people who so clearly need it. If they do come back, well perhaps they'll be ashamed.'

'Who?'

'The perverts.'

'I think we need a better plan than that.'

'Are you actually worried about our resettlers being kicked out? Or are you just worried that someone might be angry with you? That you might get told off for being a naughty girl?'

'I don't care about being told off.'

'You have to stop thinking that if you're a

good little girl then eventually someone will reward you,' says Cassandra. 'It simply doesn't work like that. Look at you — a shabby nonentity. For all your trying, you're nothing. Then look at Banker Sooke. He is a pervert. But he is a rich happy pervert. He doesn't care about you. Why do you care about him?'

'I don't care about him.'

'You won't get extra marks for being teacher's pet. You won't go to the top of the class. There is no class. There is no teacher. Or if there is then you have to understand that he or she doesn't actually like you. You are not being marked out of ten for how neatly you sharpen your pencil and how lovely your handwriting is. You are not going to get a gold star. You are not the fucking flower monitor and no one cares what you do.'

'If I break the law they care.'

'That's true. That's how to make them care. Break the damn law.'

Later they'll say I was led astray. But they'll clap me in irons all the same. I know this, I know it rationally but somehow I can't change things. I think I don't really want to. It could be suppressed rage that's fuelling my folly. Or it could be that Cassandra's right and I'm so bored rigid with my law-abiding life which never got me anywhere that anything seems better.

Even breaking and entering seems better.

15

Cassandra is wearing white. A long white robe with flowing skirts. A white hat. White gloves. Clean white shoes, not a trace of stinking mulch on either one. Her face is clean and she smells faintly of toothpaste.

In the grimy kitchen she stands there glowing like an angel and I say, 'Going somewhere nice?'

'To a funeral.'

'I'm sorry to hear that.'

She nods sternly. Then she walks out of the door, her robes rustling.

I follow her into the garden, saying, 'Who's died? Anyone I know?'

I follow her along the lane, and up the hill towards Beckfoot Cottage. 'Have Mavis and Arthur died?' I say as I trot along beside her. 'Have they?'

'Be quiet.'

'Sorry. I just wondered . . . '

'Don't wonder. Be quiet.'

So I keep quiet as we walk up the path and through the wood, where the rain is hissing on the leaves, and I follow her along the path towards Kiln Bank Farm, saying not a word until at the sheep enclosure I briefly forget myself and say, 'But aren't you going to the church?' and she hisses, 'Ssssh' at me, and I subside again. The whole thing is mysterious enough and then we arrive at the Quaker burial ground and there's a crowd of people waiting. They are all silent as Cassandra bows under the lintel and pushes open the gate.

They are villagers, and I've seen most of them around, though they've devoutly refused to speak to me. There's the woman who walks past stony-faced when we meet on the bridge, and the man who lives by the church, who steadfastly ignores me whenever he gets the opportunity. Then there's the old couple who walk hand in hand slowly along the lane each evening, who ritually avert their eyes whenever I pass them. Then a few others, all of them still unsmiling and unnodding, but now they are in their finest clothes, ties and jackets rather than the sullied boots and overalls they usually wear.

No one else, however, is wearing a robe.

No one else is wearing a large white cloth hat.

No one else is saying, 'Brothers and sisters, let us begin.'

Cassandra is saying, 'Let us remember the life of Bob Cooper, who has died at the age of sixty-two. Bob Cooper was a modest man, a good man, who always helped his family and his friends. He is survived by his son, Peter, and his daughter, Gwen. May his soul rest in the earth. May he not be perplexed by posthumous terrors. May he not be assailed by anything tedious or unacceptable in the afterlife. May he find something better than complete and unending oblivion, if there is something better, but may he not be troubled by any sort of sanctimonious deity judging him for his sins.'

There is a general murmur of agreement.

'Bob lived unsinning and he died unsinning. He lived from the land and may he now lie at peace in the land. And may his heirs continue to live from the land, as their antecedents have done for centuries and centuries before them.'

And everyone nods slowly.

'If anyone would like to add anything to the address, please feel free to speak now,' says Cassandra.

There is a long pause. Everyone stands there patiently, rain squeaking on their umbrellas, waiting in case some member of the Cooper family suddenly feels the urge to speak.

While we all wait, I stare at the fields — full of sheep — and the fells — coated in red bracken — and the black clouds above us. I stare around at all these neighbours in their sober black clothes. This is the settled community of the village. They live in the skanky modern houses, the ones the forestry commission made from concrete and the ones the perverts regard as eyesores. Or the almshouses, a row of cramped-up Victorian cottages with a parsimonious garden around them.

Normally Cassandra hardly talks to them. Perhaps she used to live it up in the local pub on a Friday night, but then the desert burned and her husband burned and I get the impression she hasn't really spoken to anyone since. From time to time she consults them on practical matters. A bull for her cow. An exchange of goods. Trouble with her mangy broken Land Rover. But they never come round. You never get the old couple who walk along the lane turning up for a cup of tea. Or Mrs Askam arriving with some cheese scones.

They respect her, but they don't really talk to her.

They leave her well alone.

Even as they pause, they are eyeing her strangely, as if they're not quite sure what to make of her.

The rain is falling harder now. Cassandra waits a few more minutes as the rain hisses on the grass and then she says, 'Thank you, brothers and sisters. And we shall not mourn Bob, not in a lachrymose or miserable way. We will celebrate him, and the land he farmed, and the house he and his parents built, and we will hold out our hands to his two children, our friends.' And everyone holds out their hands.

'Peace be with you all,' says Cassandra.

At the end everyone files up to Cassandra and thanks her and she nods and says to each of them, 'Peace be with you,' and then they all bow under the lintel and walk off down the path.

Cassandra swishes along in her robes, the hem now covered in mulch.

★　★　★

As soon as we're inside the farmhouse I say, 'What was all that about?'

'That,' she says piously, 'was about the life of Bob Cooper. Weren't you listening?'

'I didn't know you were a vicar.'

'I'm not. That wasn't a religious ceremony.'

'So why are you wearing that robe?'

'I am trained to give humanist burials.'

'That was a humanist burial?'

'Of course it was. Weren't you listening?'

She pauses for a moment, then she says,

'My husband is buried in that Quaker ground.'

'Why, are you a Quaker?'

'No, but I had to bury him somewhere. And there was no way I was letting that weird vicar get his hands on my husband. But I was very conservative then. These days I would put him deep under the cow field and have done with it. But then, I toed the line. I put him up in the Quaker burial ground because as long as you say you are a thing, a Christian or a Quaker or whatever, then people let you carry on. It's only if you say, actually I'm not anything in particular but I just want to bury my husband in my garden, that they start to get their little rulebooks out.'

'So you're not religious?'

'I am profoundly religious.'

'But you're not a Christian?'

'No, I'm aiming higher than that.'

'What's wrong with being a Christian?'

'It's a sky god religion.'

'And a sky god religion is?'

'A very bad thing.'

'I'm afraid I wasn't aware of such a strain of theology . . . '

'Those religions with their angry life-hating gods. Their autocratic sky gods. Thou shalt not. They're all just pathological.'

'You can't dismiss the beliefs of billions of

people as pathological. Can you?'

I know, the answer already.

'Of course you can,' says Cassandra. 'Lots of people like buying weird bits of furniture in Ikea. Lots of people like reading monstrous rubbish about celebrities. It's all the same. They're all pathologies, collectively suffered but pathological all the same.'

'I hardly think believing in the Christian God is like shopping in Ikea.'

'Do they know anything about their God? Do they know where he comes from? Do they care? Not at all, they just take away their flatpacked ready-made religion and install it in their lives.'

'I don't think they see it that way.'

'They don't want to see it. They don't want to see anything at all. They just want to take it and set it up. Ikea Christ, the easy-to-assemble deity.'

'OK, anyway,' I say, 'so why are you conducting funerals?'

'Because of the death duties,' she says.

'What, you get paid for it?'

'Don't be ridiculous.'

'What do you mean then?'

'Round here, people have farms and if they die suddenly or don't manage to sign the farm over to their children before they die then the farms have to be sold to pay the

155

death duties. You get people losing farms which have been in their family for hundreds of years.'

'That's very sad.'

'So I offer a practical solution. If someone dies without signing over their farm to their children, I am happy to conduct a ceremony sometime after the legal matters have been sorted out.'

'I don't understand.'

'Bob Cooper, for example, has been dead for three and a half months. But it is only last Friday that he officially died. So three months ago he signed over his farm to his eldest daughter, and now we are mourning the sudden and shocking death of Bob Cooper.'

'Where's he been since he died?'

'He's been at the burial ground.'

'Already buried?'

'Yes, of course. You wouldn't want to have had him sitting in the kitchen all these months, would you?'

'But surely his doctor knows when he really died? Or the coroner? Don't you have to get a death certificate or something?'

'Come with me.' And Cassandra leads me into her 'study', which is one of the most cluttered and shambolic of all the rooms, piled high with papers and books and the walls coated with shabby landscape prints, and she starts rummaging in a drawer. Then she produces a pile of papers and lays them out before me.

They are death certificates. Signed by the coroner, but with everything else — date, name of the deceased, and so on — left blank.

'How come you have these?' I say.

'The coroner, an old friend of mine, did them for me before he died. I have his death certificate somewhere here — oh yes, here it is.'

'The coroner is going to die on 15 August 2038,' I read flatly.

'I need his signature for as long as possible. But any longer than 2038 and he's going to be eligible for a telegram from the queen. Which would just make things complicated.'

'I assume you know just how staggeringly illegal this is? How rip-roaringly, madly, completely against the law it is to forge death certificates?'

'Once again you are touchingly convinced that we must pander to laws even when they are designed to shaft us,' she says.

She tidies up the death certificates and puts them carefully away.

'I can't believe that coroner gave you all those forged death certificates.'

'He was dying, he didn't care. What are they going to do? Pursue him to Hades and take away his licence? Tell him off? Ohhh, now you're in real trouble. Well, yes I am actually, I'm dead. No no, you're in real trouble. We're going to take you to court. Oh no, that really is bad. I thought being dead was bad, but no you're right, it's much more dreadful to be taken to court. Now I'm really quaking in my boots, except I don't have any boots, because I'm dead.'

'OK, I see why he was quite relaxed about breaking the law. But how can you be so relaxed?'

There are a thousand answers to this question. Because she genuinely doesn't care. Because she is never caught. Because she is dismissed as an eccentric widow whose husband did sterling service for his country. A devoted military wife, who couldn't cope with the grief.

'I live in the ruins of my farm, in an obscure valley,' she says. 'Why would they think I was up to anything at all?'

And for a moment I am reassured. I look across at Cassandra and I think that no one is going to suspect her. They think she's a crank. A woman who blew a gasket. They think she's busy tinkering with her windmill and baking quinoa pie and chasing her last couple of pigs around the pen and lighting the candles on a shrine to her dead husband.

They come round to rap her on the knuckles when she contravenes some water board edict or something about the disposal of waste and they see her loping along on her scrawny legs and no one, but no one, would think she was up to anything major, anything like forging death certificates or stealing houses. She's a local sight, to be explained in a tidy phrase. The mad widow on the hill.

I see this quite clearly, and for a moment I think we will be fine.

Nothing will happen to us.

16

Nothing happens for a while.

The days dawn clear and quiet and conspicuously, reassuringly, nothing happens.

The frost settles on the grass in the mornings. The sunsets are a crazy dying red. The trees weep their leaves to the ground and the branches are left looking naked and frail.

Day by day nothing happens.

Nothing happens in the mornings when we rise and nothing happens as the nights grow colder and I lie in my bed gripping the sheets and shuddering with cold.

Nothing happens as the days grow shorter and darkness seeps along the valley.

Nothing happens, except my blood blanches and I am afflicted with vile snuffling diseases.

In this deep nothing, a nothing growing fainter and more nothingish by the day, Cassandra says, 'We need more resettlers,' and somehow with my wits dulled by the nothing I say, 'OK.'

And with the nothing swirling around us, cladding us, enveloping us in nothing, Cassandra says, 'There's a new house I want you to take someone to,' and I receive the keys and go.

I go, in the Land Rover, into this consoling nothing as if I am driving off to the shops. As if I have nothing to fear. Because nothing will happen.

I drive through the nothing and at the door are some resettlers, waiting for their keys.

Thank you thank you, they say, and I shuffle round another stolen house and smile graciously and then I say, 'Enjoy your stay.'

Let us know if there's anything you need.

Thanks so much, we will, they say.

Then I drive away.

And once again, nothing happens.

Nothing happens and I do this a dozen times, maybe twenty. And eventually I am like a bored estate agent.

'Here you are. OK, right, here's the lights, the stuff, the other stuff, here's something else oh look more stuff and here are the keys.'

And off I go, the doyenne of mundane crime.

When I walk around the village I see a vista of such normality it's hard to imagine that it's all teetering on the brink of disaster. At Riverbank I see the hunched form of Irene Gibbs, watching television. Further along the road is the Old Vicarage and Matthew Yates is in the front garden, doing something to a

161

flower bed. And then there's a gap, a winding gap of road and hedgerow, sheep in the fields, the river flowing and the breeze tussling with the bracken and then there's Wilton Mill looking like an epicentre of unchanging ordinariness.

And at Wolf Barn everyone is steeped in this illusory sense of normality, though naturally they think this is indeed normal, that they are living a non-illusory nondescript life of interest to no one and perhaps they even think they have been lucky. They are all working hard because they are grateful. The ginger man is bringing in firewood. Another man called Dave has rigged up a wind turbine. A woman called Sue has mapped out a vegetable garden, and she and some others are starting to plant it. And there's a big hole in the ground where they're boring for water.

I meet Paul Bowness and he says, 'Morning. Come to inspect the troops?'

'Just thought I'd drop in,' I say.

'We haven't trashed the place yet,' he says. 'Apart from this bloody great hole.' For a moment or two we look down into the hole.

'It certainly is awfully deep,' I say.

'Who knows what's down there?' he says.

'Water, you hope.'

'We hope indeed.'

'Do you need anything?'

'We could really do with a goat, for starters.'

'You could probably have one of our goats,' I say. 'We don't really need two.'

'OK. We might club together and get some chickens,' he says.

'Or we can help with some cash.'

He has his hands in his pockets. Swaying a little, forwards and backwards.

'Did you make the big deep hole?' I say.

'I did, with the help of Danny and Ben.' He nods to two young guys, who are walking across the courtyard with spades.

'Well it's very nice,' I say. 'Well done.'

'Yes, you can't beat a bit of digging.'

Perhaps it's the immortal wit of our conversation or perhaps the profound importance of the matters we are discussing, but it seems Paul Bowness has suffered a miniature social crisis and can no longer meet my gaze. I've been hanging on for a flash glance or even a trace of the low-level flirtation that I thought I sensed last time. But nothing. Not even a meeting of eyes. Instead Paul Bowness is looking askance. He's looking at his shoes. He's looking down the bloody great hole.

'So you're finding you have everything you need?' I say.

'Yes, thanks.'

'OK,' I say doubtfully, and sidle away.

I wonder what it means. Then I think that really I have enough to worry about without speculating about the latent meaning of Paul's failure to look at me, and if he wants to be a buttoned-up freak with no social skills then that's entirely up to him.

And I won't think about it for another minute, I think.

I won't contemplate it at all.

I am deeply uninterested in the underlying significance of Paul Bowness's sudden shyness. Therefore I will not consider the matter again.

If that Swiss fellow ever does turn up, I think as I look at the rubble in the courtyard and the way they've rearranged the garden, there's going to be real hell. *Sturm und drang* won't even begin to describe it.

When I'm out of the wood and back on the path towards the road, perhaps I accidentally wonder again what was wrong with Paul Bowness and perhaps I have just pushed the thought aside when I see the old farmer coming along on his mini tractor. I am making myself small and insignificant, trying to press myself against a tree, when I look up and see there is a curious twist to his mouth and he is looking straight at me. He is staring directly at me, and what is this? What strangeness is this?

The old farmer seems to be smiling. That really does seem to be what he is doing, though it takes me a few moments to begin to comprehend it, and then — uncertainly — I smile back.

Then he's gone, through a gap in the wall to another field.

★　★　★

Nothing washes over us.

We bathe in a consoling spa of nothingness and we take the waters of nothingness each day.

At the river Cassandra points down and says, 'Just look at that.'

'At the water?'

'That, I mean,' she says, pointing at the water again.

So I look more closely and I see a shadow, something lurking under the surface.

'What is it?'

'It's a gigantic fat salmon. A huge beast. Lying there, waiting to go upstream.'

'Why is it waiting?'

'It's waiting because it's fat and greedy and all it's thinking about is sex. You could dangle the tastiest piece of bait at it for hours on end and it wouldn't bite. Until it can swim upstream, it's refusing to do anything.'

'Aren't you going to catch it?'

'Why on earth would I do that?'

'Because it's huge and we could live off it for about a month.'

'But then it wouldn't get to breed. So it would have been lying in wait all this time and it would never get its reward.'

And what is our reward, I wonder? What will happen to us at the end of all this waiting?

★　★　★

Idling waves of nothing lap against us as we sit in Beckfoot, in the living room with the flat screen before us like an oracle and all the antique oddments arrayed on Regency wood, Mr and Mrs Sooke glaring down at us from the bookshelves.

And now there are flowers on the drum table, and on the card table appears a jarring display of interpolated china dogs and glass elephants, the sort of cheap rubbish which would make the Sookes instantly nauseous, but which Mrs Williams couldn't bear to be without.

And Mavis Williams says, 'More sugar?'

'Thank you,' says Cassandra.

'Another biscuit?' says Arthur.

'Don't mind if I do,' I say.

Around us the house has been changed by occupation. No longer quite as frosty and immaculate as before. There are perhaps a few stains on the chaise longue. A careless splash of tea on the damask. A copy of the *Daily Mirror* on the rosewood stool. Thick reading glasses on top of it, regulation NHS. And the place reeks of Mavis's perfume, something overpowering and tactless like rose water and strawberries.

And Cassandra says, 'So you've settled in well, have you?'

The Williamses smile back at her. They are less bewildered than before. They seem quite at home, handing out tea and bourbon biscuits. They have set out photographs in ugly frames on the marble mantelpiece. Grandchildren, waving messily at the camera. Their daughter wearing a tracksuit.

A tracksuit! I imagine Mrs Banker Sooke saying, 'With such awful bleached hair!'

Cassandra is there in one of her shabbiest most garden-soiled jackets, her legs thrown defiantly over the arm of a chair, and I am perched on the chaise longue, thinking how Mrs Sooke probably inherited it from one of her many rich relatives, and it is worth about £35,000 but the Williamses have slopped PG Tips on it nonetheless. But perhaps it doesn't matter so much. There are plenty more chaises longues where that one came from. Of course, all Mrs Sooke's relatives are rich. Perish the thought that one of them might be a pauper. That would get them excommunicated soon enough.

And then they would be flayed.

Mavis is stirring in her sugar and saying, 'We've been so enjoying the garden.'

'I've been pruning a little bit, here and there, like you said, Cassandra,' says Arthur.

'Pruning what?' I say.

'Oh, I told the Williamses to work away in the garden, as they pleased,' says Cassandra. 'I'm sure the owners would so like to see their garden used.'

'I'm sure they would,' I say.

'Well, did they say we could?' says Arthur. It's my tone of voice, perhaps, that's made him furrow his filmy skin.

'They have offered no objections,' says Cassandra. 'They are quite relaxed about everything.'

'I really hope we can meet them one day,' says Mavis. 'I would love to meet them.'

'Well, perhaps you will,' says Cassandra.

'I would make them my best Victoria sandwich,' says Mavis.

I almost release a treacherous volley of hysterical laughter, but somehow I suppress it. I sit there with my head down, hoping my inner struggle goes unnoticed.

When I glance up, Cassandra is poker faced. 'I'm sure they would really appreciate that,' she says.

'More tea?' Mavis is saying to me.

Silently I hold out my cup.

'I like a nice sponge cake,' Arthur says. 'Delicious with cream.'

'You don't need cream for a really good one, if the sponge is really sweet and soft,' says Mavis.

'Do you not?' says Cassandra. 'That surprises me. I would have thought you would always need cream.'

'Oh no,' says Mavis. 'It's not necessary at all. Jam alone does fine. Would you like another cup of tea?'

'Don't mind if I do,' says Cassandra.

★　★　★

Later, when we are back at the farm and still nothing has happened, I say to Cassandra, 'Don't you have a feeling of suspense?'

'About what?'

'As if something must surely be about to happen?'

'Something is always about to happen.'

'No, I mean something bad.'

'What do you mean by bad?'

'I mean the owners coming back.'

'Why would that be bad?'

'Well, for the obvious reasons, surely.' And I think, surely they are obvious, even to you?

'In a sense it would be awkward. But at least the perverts would finally notice what's going on.'

'But we don't want them to notice.'

'For the sake of the resettlers, it's convenient if they don't notice. But really you would expect they would notice. Yet they seem not to care at all. It's rather insulting.'

'Don't worry, when they find out they'll care right enough.'

'They should be making more of an effort. How are we meant to sustain any sense that there is order and meaning in society, or indeed even the universe, if people can't even be bothered to notice that their houses have been stolen?'

'We're not doing this to ascertain whether the universe is meaningful are we?'

'No, our main objective is to supply people with houses. However, we have also revealed that the perverts are completely indifferent. More worrying still, we seem to have revealed that the universe is completely indifferent. We are alone in our resettlement, as we are alone in everything else.'

'Well, that's a terribly weighty conclusion

to have reached, on the basis of a few weeks,'
I say.

'The problem with you is you just try not
to think about nasty tasteless subjects like
death,' says Cassandra.

'That's not true.'

'You don't even want to imagine that you'll
die and rot and get turned into mulch. And
then somebody will spread you on their
mangolds.'

'You will, probably, when you've killed me
with stress and overwork.'

'I wouldn't put your scrawny little hide on
my mangolds. I'd be afraid that your inner
corruption would pollute my crops.'

'You're just a child. You're just childish,' I
say. For some reason this business about the
mangolds really offends me.

'You're just angry that I told you the truth,
that you will die, like everyone else.'

'I'm just angry with you anyway.'

Cassandra is smiling at me, with an
irritating triumphalist smile, the sort of smile
she emitted when she first showed me the
thunderbox.

'I told you you should get more angry,' she
says. 'I'm so glad you're finally taking my
advice.'

'You're just a sanctimonious lunatic,' I say.
We are back at the farm and I push open the

gate and march away to the pond.

As I walk I hear her shouting after me, 'There's nothing for it. You can't run away from it. Death will find you all the same! You should be angry! Be REALLY ANGRY!'

17

In the wood I meet Paul Bowness.

He's still doing that perplexing thing with the averted gaze.

The averted gaze falls on the hedgerow, moves along to scan the gate and the massing crowds of sheep. But it is studiously averse to my face.

In truth he looks as if he's weighing something up. He looks as if he knows, and he's trying to decide whether to confront us. Whether to betray us. So my guilty conscience makes me stutter as we stand there, and then there's his air of reluctance and vague embarrassment. Matters stall; our meeting is over almost as soon as it's begun.

I move along, trying to look busy. 'Hope all's well,' I shout behind me. 'Must catch up soon.'

'Yes, let's do that,' he says, in a slow, melancholy way, as if he is internally lamenting my all-round weakness of character.

That makes me wonder why Cassandra slipped up so badly, bringing in someone who might actually ask a few questions and reach the obvious conclusion that the whole thing is a tapestry of lies. A big saggy tapestry, unravelling even as we weave it.

★   ★   ★

Bracken Lodge, resettled. Seatoller Cottage, resettled. The Old Mill, resettled. Bracelet Hall, resettled. Dunnerdale House, resettled.

★   ★   ★

And Paul Bowness keeps his nose in the air, sniffing the scent. When I see him I think we should have stuck to the aged. Mavis and Arthur Williams, they don't ask snide little questions. They don't smirk tragically and say, 'More resettlers, how do you do it?' with their eyes fixed on a point to your left.

Mavis and Arthur Williams are content to know very little: they have a house, a stack of doilies, some teacakes, a fine collection of eighteenth-century furniture; they are glad.

Paul Bowness, on the other hand — it's making me wild how Paul Bowness knows. It's plain anomalous of him, irritatingly unusual, when most of them are content with a state of unknowing. They don't intend to know. Mavis and Arthur are simply delighted. The Wadsworths are another exemplary case.

Pure ignorance and gratitude. I see them in their garden and they fall over themselves trying to reach the fence. They thank me, their rheumy eyes shining. Unabridged delight. Touching in the circumstances. A little painful, but touching all the same.

'Such a wonderful thing,' they say. They abide by the rules. They make the beds every morning. They are careful as they walk around the house. They clean everything incessantly. They tidy and give thanks whenever they see me.

And I wonder if Paul thinks it's worse than it is, if he believes I've murdered the owners and stolen their houses.

★ ★ ★

Forest Cottage, resettled. Miller's Howe, resettled. Yew Tree Farm, resettled.

★ ★ ★

I go down to Wolf Barn to deliver a goat. I am leading Descartes along, and when I reach the yard a woman called Mandy says, 'That's a fine goat.'

'It's yours.' I hand her the tether.

'Thank you,' she says, less admiring now she has the smelly beast beside her.

'Descartes, meet Mandy.'

Mandy has long straight hair and the atmosphere of the village fete hanging off her, and she would be outraged if she knew what was really happening. She's something of a hippy but not one who wants to get slammed in prison. A peaceable, authority-respecting organic-food-buying type of hippy, not a man-the-barricades and smash-the-pigs type. As she's standing there wondering what to do with the goat and I'm wondering whether Paul is going to appear, Mandy says to me, 'Can I ask you something?'

That makes me wonder what she knows, but she says, 'I heard that Cassandra White calls the owners perverts. Why does she do that?'

And I say, 'I'm sure she's never used a word like that.'

Mandy nods respectfully and then she says, 'And is it true that Cassandra White cursed God and then after she had cursed God her husband was killed and her farm was blighted with disease?'

'You shouldn't believe everything you hear, you know.'

She says, as if I haven't spoken at all, 'But is it true that she's a druid?'

Through my sardonic smile I say it sounds as if Mandy should talk to Cassandra herself,

176

as she seems to be so curious about her, and she blushes and says, 'Oh no, I wouldn't want to bother her with my insignificant questions.'

And she goes away, dragging Descartes behind her.

★ ★ ★

Paul is nodding to the ground and explaining that he's been doing something to the electrics.

'The place looks amazing but the guy was shafted completely by some local electrician.'

'I suppose it hasn't mattered for a while,' I say.

'Well, he's hardly been in danger of electrocuting himself, out there in Basel or wherever he is.'

'Found any water yet?'

'No, we went really far down and we only found salt,' he says.

'Well, you'll have to keep trying,' I say.

'We need better equipment,' he says. 'Really, we need more money.'

'The point of this all is to subsist on very little money,' I say. 'You have to tighten your belts.'

And he nods and stares off stage left and says, 'All in a good cause.' I'm wondering if I should say something about the weighty sense of unease, the plain embarrassment squatting on our conversation but then the ginger-haired man turns up and says they have to do something to a fence, and Paul says, 'Sorry, I should go. See you soon.'

I see Mandy approaching with the goat and before she can try to give it back I walk away.

It works away at me as I walk back through the wood, as I retrace my steps along the road and past the resettled houses.

I think about it all evening, and I say to Cassandra, 'That guy Bowness knows,' and she says, 'Who cares? Let him know.'

*   *   *

I rise thinking about his knowingness and I go to milk the goat thinking about his sorrowful forgiving expression and his averted eyes as if he can't bear to contemplate my sin and then I pile manure onto the garden thinking all the time that if the cunning fucker knows, why doesn't he leave, and stop looking like a penitent priest who's been dumped in with a pile of warty heathens, and then I bring in vegetables and store them and all the time I'm thinking that Paul Bowness can go and hang himself because there's no way I care what he thinks or what he knows.

Cassandra is plainly untouchable, the

queen in her castle, even if her castle is a stinking old farmhouse with creaking beams and a garden piled with dung.

I am the ordinary factotum, and that means when the central heating gets bust, the resettlers come and find me.

Or when they need more firewood, or when there's been an argument at Wolf Barn about whose turn it is to get the eggs.

One night Mavis Williams needs a cup of sugar, so she comes into the kitchen and finds Cassandra there alone. And she says — I hear it because I'm just in the next room — 'I'm so sorry to bother you, Mrs White. Is your assistant there?'

★ ★ ★

As I scuttle around tending to their needs they ask me — in hushed whispers, lest they be punished for speaking her name —

Is Cassandra White the best rider in the valley, and can she ride over the fells blindfolded and with her hands tied behind her back?

Can she run from here to the Hardknott Pass in half an hour?

And is she the best shot in the valley and can she shoot a hare from two hundred paces in the dark?

And can she slaughter a cow with her bare hands?

And does she bathe once a year in the blood of her pigs?

★ ★ ★

'I do all the work and they revere you like a god,' I say to Cassandra one day when we are together in the store cupboard.

'I do all the thinking. The thinking is the real work,' says Cassandra.

'But I actually deal with the crap,' I say.

'They need someone like you. And then they need someone like me — or what they think I am.'

'Well I'd rather be you than me.'

'I don't think you would,' she says.

And she lifts up her head and laughs. 'I don't think you would at all.'

★ ★ ★

And is it true that Cassandra White has six fingers on one hand?

Can she see into people's souls and judge what she sees?

And is she old, terribly old, more than eighty though she looks so young?

Can she see the future and, if so, does she

know that we are going down?

We are going down and then we are going further down and then oh we are going a little further down again.

★ ★ ★

Ivy House resettled. Quarry Bank resettled. Birch Tree Farm resettled. Pig Hoof Cottage resettled. Recently renovated former hovel resettled. Itchy Cow Cottage resettled. Biting Midge Cottage resettled.

★ ★ ★

Detective Bowness comes walking along the path. Detective Bowness with his grand theory, and eventually he'll stand us both in a room and say, 'You have been clever, ladies, but not quite clever enough . . . '

Cassandra just shrugs and laughs. She shrugs it off. 'Stop thinking about Paul Bowness,' she says.

'I'm not thinking about him, I'm thinking about what he knows,' I say.

'Really?' she says. 'Is there a difference?' And she goes back to the garden laughing and nodding her head.

18

This time at Wolf Barn I know I will confront him. I have an elegant frosty exchange in mind.

Me at the door, knocking efficiently, Paul Bowness answering, me saying, in a high-minded wounded tone, 'Is there something you want to ask me?' and him saying, 'What do you mean?' and me saying, 'If you have something you want to say just say it,' and him perhaps suddenly aghast, realising I am not to be toyed with, and saying, 'I have been unjust, I realise, and I have not allowed you to present your side of the story,' and me saying, with a catch in my throat, 'We have only thought of others, all our thoughts have been with others,' and him saying, 'I understand the inherent goodness of your actions and I am so very sorry I ever judged you badly,' and finally him saying, 'Perhaps I might shake you by the hand, to express my profound admiration for your courage,' and cut to sonorous stirring music.

The reality is somewhat different.

I knock on the door and Mandy answers,

clad in lank brown hair. Flipping it around as she calls Paul's name into the echoing interior. There is a gaping silence and then he appears, wiping his hands.

'Good morning,' he says. 'Some resettlement business?'

'Yes, you might say so.'

'How's all that resettling going?' he says, and he's smiling at something — the piano, or perhaps the fireplace.

'Very well,' I say.

We stand there for a moment while he maintains an embarrassed smile and I try to maintain my dignified fury, then I say, 'Paul can we go somewhere private? I have to talk to you about something.'

He says, stammering slightly, 'Let's go upstairs. There's no one there during the day.'

Most of the rooms upstairs are bedrooms but there's an elegant study on one side and so he takes me in there and says, 'Make yourself at home.'

I sit down in an armchair and I look closely at him — at his sandy hair and his red skin, and his flush of health and strength.

For a moment he is silent, then he says, 'Well, so, you have something you want to talk about?'

'Well really I think there's something you

183

want to say to me, isn't there, Paul?'

He looks startled at this bold note and for a moment he doesn't reply. Then he says in a soft voice, a reluctant voice with a nervous edge, 'Well, you may have noticed that I am a bit unnatural with you. That I find it hard to talk to you.'

'I have noticed,' I say. Now I'm expecting the grand accusation. *You have been very foolish indeed. I have a good mind to go straight to the police.*

'I'm sorry if it's so obvious.'

'It's OK.'

'I think it's because I fancy you,' he says, and now he looks straight at me. I have already opened my mouth to say *I can explain everything* and then I close it again.

'Ah,' I say. 'Oh.'

I wonder if he is joking, if there is a custom here to humiliate the already fallen by such blatant lies, and I am preparing to be a good sport, to smirk away with my cheeks aching while he says, 'Fooled you . . . hah . . . ' But then he appears to be kissing me, in a far from satirical manner, or if this is satire then I must spend more time reading the works of Swift and Pope and then he takes my hand and leads me into his bedroom and on a maxi-luxury emperor-sized bed we hurl our clothes around and when he is naked before me I am nearly convinced it isn't a joke.

Creak creak goes the bed, the maxi-comfort bed. Creak that we shall know the meaning of bliss. Bliss beyond all bliss before. Bliss that passes all previous understanding of bliss that redefines the notion of bliss or certainly the inadequate patchwork notion I had of bliss

That we shall know the meaning of CREAK

CREAK

Jesus Creak, I say

And all the angels

CREAK the cherubim and A — men . . .

There is a pulse in my neck beating faster and faster.

And Paul says, 'Oh My God,' and I say, 'Fuck' and he says, 'Jesus Fuck' and then there is silence except for the energetic contribution of the bed.

That we shall know the meaning of ecstasy. Ecstasy that goes beyond all ecstasy previously imagined. An ecstasy of ecstasies, ecstasy coursing into ecstasy into ecstasy into ecstasy Aaaa — men . . .

And let us sing our song of pure ecstasy, with a rousing chorus of praise to the maxi-comfort maxi-fuck bed.

* * *

185

Then we sleep and when we wake he strokes my hair and says, 'Well I think I've shirked my duties this afternoon.'

And I say, 'It's funny, when I came round I thought you were going to say something else.'

'I know what you thought I was going to say.'

'What?'

'You thought I was going to tell you I knew about resettlement, that it's not true.'

'Yes.'

'Well, of course I know. But I don't care.'

'Really?'

'Not at all.'

★   ★   ★

And I walk back to the farm thinking of him and the feel of his hands and his long firm legs and the smell of him and the feel of him and

Oh did I mention the smell of him

And I lift my head and look at the stars swirling and think of his long firm legs and the smell of him and I am under the stars thinking how surprising, how unlikely, and then I catch a glimpse of Cassandra waiting in the doorway saying, 'Where in the name of Christ have you been?'

19

Cassandra takes it surprisingly well.

Really she doesn't care at all. She listens impatiently as I say, 'I have to tell you something it seems fair to tell you as I live in your house but today Paul Bowness and I became more than friends' — not that we were friends before in fact — 'and I think the situation of being more than friends may perhaps be ongoing though of course we'll be discreet,' and she says, 'Never mind, it doesn't matter now because we have another house to resettle tomorrow. The resettler is Max Greyson, who is living in just such a dump, you should see it. The place sent me raging mad. Just a slum, and he's been renting it since he gave his farm to his children. It's not the fault of his children, they've had a tough year. But that house is shocking. I went round and thought well there's that house over Birker Fell, that would do, a bit isolated but we can send up food and wood from time to time, and bring him down here for dinner a couple of times a week, what do you think?'

'OK,' I say.

'Good. Oh, the cow needs her evening milking, so can you do it and I'll make dinner?'

'OK,' I say.

I am feeling fairly crushed as I walk across the yard. I remain crushed as I grab the cow's dug and milk it dry. Then I go to the thunderbox and that kills any remaining trace of sensual pleasure.

★ ★ ★

Over dinner — pheasant, winter cabbage, turnips, carrots, potatoes — I say, 'By the way Paul Bowness knows.'

'Knows what?'

'He knows resettlement is a lie. He knew from the start.'

'He was bound to,' Cassandra says. 'He won't care anyway.'

'He says he doesn't.'

'He's hardly blameless. He's been poaching from the estates for years.'

'Really? Poaching?'

'Of course. They breed up millions of game birds and then they're too fat and lazy to shoot them. So then they send out their gamekeepers to cull them. Paul is just doing them a favour. Saving the gamekeepers' time.'

'Very kind of him.'

'This pheasant, that's one of Paul's.'

I look at it again. On my fork, this pheasant which came from Paul's hand, the same hand which . . . but then Cassandra says, 'Tomorrow we have to get the cow into the cowshed. And we need a great big manure session in the garden. Are you up for it?'

'Manure, OK, great,' I say.

'And, by the way — ' she says.

And I think now, now she will say something about me and Paul, about what I told her earlier. I wait, thinking perhaps she will be angry after all, or wounded, perhaps she will feel the exclusivity of our friendship is under threat from such a relationship, and I wait to console her, to explain that I am still dedicated to her and to the cause, as dedicated as ever, and she says — 'Don't ever leave the door to the woodshed open again. The rainstorm this afternoon half soaked all our supplies.'

And I think, what rainstorm? I never heard the rain.

20

The salmon have floated away. And Cassandra is bellowing through the house.

The perverts are coming, she is bellowing.

'It's the Old Vicarage,' she says. 'Chrissie at the shop phoned me. She does the cleaning for them and the pervert owners phoned yesterday to say they're coming today and can she dash in this morning and do a quick clean for them.'

'How lucky they phoned her,' I say, but I can hardly think. All I can think is PERVERTS. HERE. HERE. PERVERTS.

'Anyway, you have to go and get Matthew and Tabitha out,' Cassandra is saying.

'I have to?'

'Yes, take them to Beckfoot.'

'But what if the perverts come while I'm there?'

'Then we revert to Plan B.'

'What is Plan B?'

'I'll tell you when I've thought of it.'

So I turn up my collar and stumble along the path, breathing in lungfuls of misty air. I am trying to calm myself as I cross the bridge and then I start running along the road to the left. I run past the other resettled houses, with all their tactful signs of inhabitation, smoke rising from the chimneys and a discreetly parked car or two and then I arrive at the impassive wrought-iron gates of the Old Vicarage.

Only then do I realise just how bad this is going to be.

Tabitha and Matthew, old man and woman with withered faces, start by wringing their hands. 'But it's such short notice,' they say. Then they continue with a bout of trembling and then they collect themselves a little and Matthew says, 'Do we have to clear out absolutely everything?' and I say, 'Yes, everything.' It's simply unfortunate, I explain, that the owners have been so disorganised. But part of the whole resettlement deal, I add, is that the owners would really rather the house was completely empty when they returned. We should really defer to their wishes, as they are being so very kind. (And by the way we must remember not to speak to our oh so very kind benefactors. We must actually cross the road, if we see them. It is very important we in no way communicate with the owners at all.)

They are looking at me in hardly surprising confusion as I say, 'Anyway it's unfortunate but you have an hour to pack up your things.

I'm going to get someone to help you carry them over to your temporary interim accommodation at Beckfoot.'

'Only an hour?' they're saying. They've been labouring under the tragic delusion that this is actually their home. They are looking round at their living room and their lovely multi-channel TV and they are thinking of their bedroom upstairs with their clothes neatly hanging in the wardrobe. All Tabitha's indestructible pleated skirts and Matthew's nylon shirts, encased within the finest oak the rich could buy. I tell them I'm sorry for the inconvenience. But there's nothing I can do, I add.

'Well, then we'll have to do our best,' says Tabitha bravely.

But it'll take them a day just to pack their bags, I think.

★   ★   ★

Legs buckling under a deep sense of pending doom I run through the woods. I run into the courtyard at Wolf Barn ignoring all the diligent occupants who are busy with their wells, or their bramble clearing, or their cider making or their speculations about whether Cassandra is really a water spirit or whatever they're doing, and I hammer on the door.

Again it's answered by Mandy, moving in hippy time, and by the time she's found Paul I have descended a stage further into panic and as soon as he appears I say, 'Cassandra had a call and you have to help me.' Even in the depths of my panic I find myself thinking how his mouth is shining as if he's just licked it, and then he says, 'Come in, come in, I was just thinking about you.'

In my defence I certainly try. I say, 'They're going to be here really soon, and the Yateses are packing but they'll never do it, so can you come now,' but now Paul takes my hand and says, 'How have you been?' and begins to kiss me, and then we're walking upstairs, and on the landing he says, 'I've been thinking about you all the time,' and then in his bedroom he says, 'Can I help you with this?' And he's referring to my coat, and then he's referring to my boots, and then my trousers and in a last attempt I say, 'Paul, I'm serious, I have something to tell you,' but I'm not serious at all by then, my thoughts are mangled entirely and there is only the faint murmur of sex between us, and all the while time is passing.

How much time I don't know because I'm

in a pure state of bodily freefall, and at one level it's entirely ridiculous but then the body has its tyrannical sense of propriety and correctness and my body at that moment perceives this as quite correct and proper that Paul Bowness, a man I barely know, should be here in his bare flesh before me. It is frankly incongruous if I think of the old ugh ueeergh thank God that's over sort of encounters I was having with my husband. The passion-free grinding of bodies. I am trying not to think of it, but the spectre looms briefly and inevitably, the significant contrast, and then I dismiss it forever.

'I'm meant to tell you something,' I say. In the deepest darkest heart of the act, the hammering heart, I try to muster a sentence. 'What is it, I can't quite remember. It's something . . . It's something important . . . '

'Well, then you must tell me,' he whispers.

'Oh, what is it . . . I can't quite . . . '

'Take your time . . . '

'That's it, they're coming today.'

'Who's coming?'

'The . . . how do you call it . . . the vicar.'

'Christ, don't talk about vicars, not now . . . '

'No no, not the vicar, I didn't quite mean . . . '

194

'Perhaps it's better if we don't speak.'

'But I had to tell you about the . . . the . . . '

'Really, don't tell me. It's fine.'

'But . . . '

'Tell me later . . . '

'No no I really have to tell you now, if I can just . . . '

'Don't tell me anything at all . . . '

. . . and the mounting ascending accelerating OM OM of all things and to OM we go, and a final broad resounding agricultural grunt and there is a moment where nothing happens, we are just somewhere, not doing much at all, and then I remember.

'FUCK,' I say, scrambling to get out of the bed, trying to find my clothes.

'What's wrong?'

'We have to go to the Old Vicarage.'

'Oh yes, that thing you were saying about the vicar.'

'No no no,' I say, and when I finally explain he grabs his jeans and says, 'OK, we'd really better GO.'

★ ★ ★

We arrive to find the Yateses meandering hopelessly from room to room. They are picking up things in a futile indecisive way and then dropping them. The whole place stinks of futility and indecision and their suitcases are almost empty.

At the sight of them my first impulse is to weep. Then I think perhaps Paul and I should just run for it and leave them there, because they look so confused that it would be hard for anyone to be angry with them. Surely the owners will pity them, I think, Tabitha Yates with her thin white hair all tumbling down, her pins amok and then Matthew Yates, who has no hair at all, not even a dusting, not the faintest paltry scrap, who peers through his glasses and constantly clears his throat. Who could punish these tattered old people, I think, and I am close to convincing myself that the best thing to do would be to abandon them.

That's Plan B for you, I am thinking, and I am all ready to go but Paul has another idea. He has another Plan B altogether, a less imaginative Plan B which involves actually helping them.

He is ushering them from room to room, holding out a suitcase and persuading them to fill it. They pile in their clothes, sending up a mingled smell of sweet perfume and mothballs and weird little bags of lavender tied with bits of ribbon. Then Paul takes each suitcase downstairs. In half an hour he's done the whole thing.

'So sorry if we've inconvenienced you,' I say as we pass the cleaning woman in the living room. I recognise her from Bob Cooper's funeral, and she gives me a wink when I go past.

I wait a few metres down the road with the Yateses and their bags, while Paul runs to Cassandra for the Land Rover. I wait with my stomach in a taut knot.

The Yateses are still saying, 'But really it would be so nice to meet them, just to thank them,' and I am explaining again, the explanation that makes no sense because it is plainly nonsensical, that the owners would really rather not, that they expressly requested that there should be no meetings, no acknowledgements, no thanks at all, and Tabitha Yates is saying, 'It just seems so strange, just to sneak out and not even to say hello.'

'We could have given them tea when they arrived,' says Matthew Yates, and I think yes that would have been simply charming.

When Paul arrives, we sling the cases into the Land Rover. I've only just managed to get the Yateses into the back, for all their elderly fussing and inevitable lack of a sense of urgency, when I see a big black SUV cruising along the road. Paul and I stand there watching as it slows down and then creams in through the Old Vicarage gates.

'There they are,' I say.

'Bastards,' says Paul.

★ ★ ★

Later Cassandra is waiting in the yard and when she sees us she says, 'Where the hell have you been? Did they catch you and torture you? Did you tell them everything?'

'No, we just missed them,' says Paul.

'Well, where have you been?'

'I had to pack up the Yateses' things,' says Paul.

'Then we had to drop them off at Beckfoot and spend hours helping them to unpack. Then we had to endure a tea-making session, with the Williamses fumbling around with cups and saucers and the Yateses saying perhaps they might send some flowers to the owners of the Old Vicarage while they're here,' I add.

'Yes, that would be a lovely idea,' says Cassandra. 'I'm sure they'd really appreciate it.'

'Anyway, once we'd persuaded them not to do that, and drunk a few dozen cups of tea, we came straight back here,' I say.

'Well, thanks,' says Cassandra. 'While you're here, Paul, you might as well help me butcher a pig.'

'All right,' says Paul.

And they go off to find a nice sharp knife.

21

The man at the door had a ferrety embarrassed look on his face. He scraped his boots a dozen times before he entered, then he ducked into the kitchen and stood there, looking at Cassandra and me in surprise and even perhaps disappointment. I could see why — Cassandra was looking particularly wild and dirty, with her orange flame-head and her stringy limbs, and I was picking a scab on my shoulder and wearing mangy slippers.

'Yes? How can we help?' said Cassandra.

'I was looking for the people who run the resettlement scheme,' he said.

'Who told you to come?' said Cassandra.

'Morris Byrne, at the almshouses.'

'Oh, he did, did he?'

A pause while Cassandra assessed him — his battered waterproof smelling of sweat and grease, and his pockmarked skin, and his matted curly hair, and the whole ravenous uncertain look of him.

She looked him up and down for a while and then she said, 'Yes, we are the people. In fact my colleague here is really in charge,' and

I was about to protest when the man turned to me and said, 'I really need some help.'

Then he began to cry.

It turned out his name was George and he'd made a fine old fist of things. A sort of a marital-breakdown-and-accompanying-alcoholism fist, with added redundancy and estranged children just to make things that little bit worse. And he had some sort of problem, a nervous twitch so that he kept turning his head round to look at the door. At first I thought he was waiting for a friend, but it was just an incessant spasm in the muscles, and each time he did it he tutted in frustration, fully aware I suppose that he looked like a grade A weirdo.

'I've pulled myself up by my boot straps,' he said, but he didn't look like he'd pulled himself up anywhere.

'I can't get a job. I can't find anything. I've tried everywhere. So if you want someone to chop firewood, or muck out pigs, or anything like that, I'll do it,' he said.

'Well, there's room at Wolf Barn isn't there?' said Cassandra over by the stove.

'Yes, there's a bit of room,' I said. 'But we need you to work, George. We'll give you a room in a house, but the deal is you have to work.'

'Just a roof over my head,' said George. 'I'll work my arse off.'

'That's what we like to hear, George,' said Cassandra. 'My colleague will show you to your accommodation.'

I wondered if it was better, after all, when she called me her assistant.

★   ★   ★

I am walking through the forest with George in unabridged and quite restful silence, though even as we walk he keeps snapping his head round like a schizoid owl, but I'm ignoring that well enough and noticing that there's frost on the puddles and on the branches of the trees. The year is getting cold and I can't remember the last time I saw a blue sky. Every day, the sky is white. Bold white and then smeared white and then grey white, but always some shade of white.

It tangles with your wits in the end. You can't keep waking up to a white sky, and retain any sense of judgement. I'm thinking about how I would love to go somewhere with a big bold blue sky, get out of this pale old stinking valley where I've burgled so many houses and I'm wondering if Paul would come with me when George starts stuttering away about something. I'm trying to ignore him until he says, 'People talk about your scheme all over the place. I heard someone talking about it in Millom the other day.'

'Millom? Who was talking about it in Millom?'

'Someone in a garage. I was just buying some fags. I heard a man talking about a scheme in the Duddon Valley, to put people in unused second homes.'

'You heard a man talking?'

'Yes. Isn't that amazing? I wouldn't be surprised if you didn't get the media coming down to see what's going on. Then it might catch on. They might make it a national — what's the word? — phenomenon . . . '

That chills my blood swiftly enough. I experience a deep spasm of unadulterated horror and then when the initial shock has passed I say, 'George, you must never speak to anyone about the resettlement scheme. Our main policy is privacy. Err . . . secrecy. No one must talk about it.'

He nods, then he shakes his head, because he's started twitching again. So it's impossible to tell if he understands or not.

At Wolf Barn I hand George over to Mandy as if I am presenting her with a dying rat and ask her to find him a room.

'This is George,' I say. 'He's new.'

'Hello, George.'

'Hello,' says George, snapping his head

round a few times.

'He says he wants to work,' I say.

And George thanks me and seizes my hand, while I say, 'Remember what I told you, George? Remember?' He snaps his head round to check with his imaginary friend and I think that if we are now dependent on the discretion of George then we are doomed.

Perhaps I am breathing a little fast and there's no doubt that I feel a brimming sense of nausea, but other than that my body is entirely within my control. Perhaps I have an urge to break George's nose, but that's a mere urge which I suppress almost as soon as it comes upon me. I'm a perfect model of stoicism as I walk with Paul under the damp trees.

The trees are shining in their cold slickness and the air is full of frost.

The valley is closing down, everything has gone cold and white for winter.

I'm impressing myself with my fortitude as we pass through the woodcutter's yard, where there's a wholesome stench of damp sawdust. A cockerel is crowing as we pass. Then the road turns uphill and I think, Ah well, it doesn't much matter. So they're talking about us in Millom. So the police may be here any day. What does it matter?

Paul says, 'You're very quiet today,' and I

say, 'Oh, just things, you know.'

We sink into silence again, until we emerge onto a blasted piece of moorland, complete with its indigenous gathering of long-eared sheep.

'Is this what you were going to show me?' I say, gesturing at all the dead bracken and the barren trees.

'No, not there yet,' says Paul.

'You're being very secretive.'

'It's easier to show you than explain.'

I'm trying hard to focus my thoughts elsewhere, to admire the torn-up landscape, to contemplate the babbling brooks and crashing waterfalls and the first snows on the tips of the mountains, but now it seems I don't have so much self-restraint after all, because I say in a plaintive urgent voice, all of a sudden, 'We are going to get caught.'

Once I've said it I want to scream.

'Caught by who?' says Paul.

'By anyone. Everyone.' And I tell him about George.

'That's nothing.' He laughs. 'The postman said to me the other day, 'Are you building a town in the woods?' And then he smiled at me and winked.'

'Well that's just another catastrophe.'

'I don't think so. The postman's onside. He won't tell anyone.'

'What about the random bloke in the garage? Who's he told?'

'Anyone. Everyone.'

We have turned off the road and now we're going uphill again, along the edge of a forest. It's a busy, violent plateau, all the trees waving their branches about, and our clothes flapping like sails and the wind spilling noise around us.

★　★　★

Everyone knows.

Everyone and twitching George.

We are at the mercy of gossip and the end could come any day.

Even though I've been Madam Pessimism the mistress of the doleful prediction since the beginning, I'm still not prepared for the fait accompli when it comes. It shocks me as much as if I'd been carefree and unaware of danger. Clearly my pessimism was more like the sort of 'This plane is going to crash' thoughts you have when you are waiting to take off.

'This plane is going to crash. I'm quite convinced it's going to crash. What's that noise? What's that smell? My God, it IS about to crash . . . '

But you don't really believe it will.

If it did actually turn its nose down and fall out of the sky you'd be as shocked as the next man, the one who fell into a blissful sleep as the plane taxied to the runway.

★ ★ ★

I look over at Paul. He has big boots on, and they make his legs look even longer and leaner. They make him look powerful and spare. His hair is fair and wavy and ruffled by the wind. There's no doubting my lust. Beyond that we hardly know each other. Our meeting has been so out of the ordinary, the circumstances, the general ambience. I can't imagine how it would be, were things normal and generally legal, were we living through the days in a small house in a nondescript town, popping out to the shops and paying our bills. Morning, dear. Cup of tea? Off to work? See you later? Hello, dear. Good day? Did you pick up any loo roll? Make sure to buy me some Immac hair removal cream when you next pop to the shops. Thanks so much dear . . .

And would we gradually descend into eurgh eurgh thank God that's over again?

I am getting myself vaguely worked up about the transience of pure passion, its fragility, the damaging effects of too much reality and then, with a sick sinking feeling deep in my belly I think, why bother worrying about this, when in a couple of months you'll be in jail anyway?

You'll be in a dull grey cell in your own private silence, and Paul will be somewhere else entirely.

Perhaps in his own dull grey cell.

Perhaps they'll let you write.

Dear Paul,
Will you wait for me I will wait for you I dun a picture for you here it is all my luv . . .

'Perhaps the key is to make capture as confusing as possible for the captor,' I say. 'If it is inevitable that we should get caught, then we should pose a puzzle to those who are going to catch us. The puzzle of what to do with us.'

'You're starting to sound like Cassandra.'

'How do you punish Mavis and Arthur Williams? How do you slam the poor Yateses in prison?'

'People would think it was a crying shame if you put the Yateses in prison,' says Paul.

'Especially when they don't have the faintest idea what's happening to them.'

'Especially then.'

'We need more pensioners. We need more people who are completely innocent and pitiable.'

'Or perhaps we should just tell everyone and have done with it,' says Paul.

'Tell everyone? Are you mad?'

'All the resettlers I mean.'

'I'm not sure that's the best idea.'

He shrugs and says nothing.

The wind is bawling in my ear, and ahead of us is a ruined house, barely standing on the barren slope. It's a truly smashed-in abandoned place. The walls are falling down. There are holes in the roof. The place has cavalierly surrendered to the wind and the rain, and all around are blasted tracts of empty land.

'This is what I wanted to show you,' says Paul.

Frith Hall: a big ruin with superb views. Needing only the slightest refurbishment, a new roof, some windowpanes, a bit of a rebuild. More ruin than house, if we're being precise. More gap than wall, more air than stone. But marvellous potential. Simply steeped in potential. Superb views of the valley spreading towards the coast, and then the rising lines of mountains, all the way to Eskdale.

A splendid battered house.

Inside the walls we find a draughty hall and the remains of a great hearth. Rafters with bats spilling out of them. Holes for windows, without glass. Holes for the wind to bawl through.

The ground is covered in fallen branches and bat dung and sheep droppings and nature has nearly colonised the place.

'A delightful country residence,' I say. 'In need of a certain degree of modernisation.'

'It used to be a coaching inn,' says Paul. 'That's all I know about it.'

'The house retains the original fireplace, which merely needs a little pointing to the slate, or really a full-on reconstruction of the gaping abyss where there was once a chimney.'

'I think we should resettle it.'

'Are you serious?'

'It's been ruined and empty for as long as I remember. If I get one of the lads to do the wall then I can come up here with some mates and get a roof on it. We can have it all done in a few weeks.'

'Isn't it going to be a huge job?'

'Not really. Anyway, there's already somewhere to keep cattle,' and Paul gestures to a ruined shed some metres away.

Well, I think. Well, if we could do it . . .

Then let Wolf Man come back and howl for

his Barn. Let the perverts reclaim their pervert dwellings. You could house a hundred people in this ruin.

'But who actually owns it?'

'Andrew Fairleigh bought all this land after the war. He was a good man, he had been in the navy and he used to walk around the valley saying hello to everyone. Everyone liked him. He knew how to talk to people, how to take the time to get to know them. But then he died and his son inherited everything. And his son lives down south and never comes here. He has a land manager, but basically he does very little with it.'

'So would anyone notice?'

'Well, I don't know. Hardly anyone comes up here, as far as I know.'

I am standing on a hillside by a ruined house, and what the hell, I am thinking. Why not? You can't make matters worse anyway. Matters are quite bad enough already.

'OK, let's do it,' I say.

22

The perverts are suspicious.

The Old Vicarage is empty again, but we find it has been fitted with a new set of security locks. There are bolts everywhere and every window has an alarm on it.

There's a big flashing SECURITY SYSTEM on the wall, which instantly phones the police if anyone sets it off.

We go round fully expecting to have the Yateses back in there in a day, but we find the whole place barred against us.

'How unfriendly of them,' says Cassandra.

'What made them do it?' I say.

'You were clearly careless,' says Cassandra.

'Well, we didn't have much time.'

'Mrs Yates must have left one of her curlers under the bed.'

I can imagine their horror. Mrs Pervert lifting up the fou fou, the floo floo, to pick up her diamond earring and finding — 'OH MY GOD' — a pair of false teeth.

'What is the meaning of this?'

Fainting clean away.

★　★　★

In Cassandra's study there is a pile of papers and notebooks and bitten-down pencils, and there is a chart with all the writing blurred by the damp, which says, 'Current state of resettlement: Duddon Valley'. In an inquisitive moment, when Cassandra is out roaming the fells, I notice that under an unruly pile of papers there's another chart I haven't seen before, which says, 'Current state of resettlement: Langdale Valley'. And another: 'Current state of resettlement: Eskdale Valley'. And there are lists on both, of houses and people, movingly united through the grace of Cassandra.

Then I see another folder.

'Wales,' it says.

'WALES?' I say later, when Cassandra returns.

Cassandra looks up from her pile of papers.

'Yes, the Welsh feel it's an excellent idea,' she says casually.

'Which Welsh?'

'Oh just a few Welsh friends. They're very excited about it.'

'When did this start?'

'Oh, quite recently. When the time was right.'

'Did we discuss it?'

'I'm sure we did.'

* * *

Cassandra has disciples at her feet. There's an eager little band that comes every day to the farm, asking for things to do.

'If you must, then go and bring in some vegetables,' she says to one. 'And you, now you're here you might as well make yourself useful in the store. And you, can you make cheese?'

And the disciple shakes his head mournfully, as if he would readily impale himself if it would atone for his lack of cheese-making skills.

'Oh, all right then, go and get some of the shitty straw from the cowshed,' and the little sap bounds off, dribbling with gratitude.

The farm is full of them, toady acolytes lifting hoes and ladling piles of manure and pouring from house to garden and back again, receiving instructions.

And Cassandra roars, 'You have been drawn into a battle. Anyone here who feels they were deceived, they should go now.'

She says that to a cluster of followers, a real pile of her most dedicated acolytes, and they nod and say solemnly, 'We want to stay.'

Not a single one puts up a hand, and says, 'Eeer, actually, eeeek, I think I might . . . you know . . . eeeer . . . eeek . . . bugger off . . . '

They know the truth, this small cluster, and yet they stay anyway.

Improbably, they stay.

★ ★ ★

'Where will we put the Yateses?' I say.

'Oh, keep them up at Beckfoot. There's plenty of room for them all,' she says. 'They can have the Chinese room.'

★ ★ ★

They send offerings. From the garden of Beckfoot comes a bunch of flowers. From the Wolf Barn complex, goat's milk, cheese, cider. From some outlying house in the Esk Valley, which I have never been to, there comes an entire hamper stuffed with home-grown things, which Cassandra opens with a regal nod.

And from some Welsh valley a crumbling cheese.

And from Cornwall a box of fudge.

'Cornwall?' I say.

'Did they have to send fudge?' says Cassandra.

The gifts come daily, diverse packages that make the postman wink.

This is indeed the postman who now delivers post to our resettlers at their resettled addresses. Happily handing over letters addressed to Mrs Tabitha Yates, Beckfoot, without even a c/o Pervert Sooke on them.

The postman winks and says, 'Good morning, ladies, quiet day at the farm?'

★ ★ ★

Cassandra tells her people, 'The top and bottom of the valley are being watched by our allies. Mrs Morgan at Hardknott Cottage and old Terry Willis at the foot of the valley. That means you get a warning, either way. When the thing finally crashes into crap, they'll give us a call. It takes fifteen minutes for an average man, woman or pervert to drive from old Terry Willis's house to White Farm, twenty-two minutes to drive here from Hardknott Cottage.'

They nod, they note it all down, as if they are at an evening class, as if they are leaning how to cook a perfect pasta sauce or the best way to *flamber*.

'Remember,' says Cassandra. 'You are fighting a war. You need to set up defences around your houses. You need a whole system of booby traps. Wires slung across the garden. Buckets suspended on the tops of doors.

Nothing is too base or slapstick. Things for them to fall into. Ideally you want a nice man-sized pit right by the front gate. The pervert enters. The pervert falls. The pervert is trapped five metres underground. If you do catch a pervert then call me instantly and I'll tell you what to do with them.'

'What will you tell them to do with them?' I ask her later.

'I haven't decided yet.'

*　*　*

I am at Frith Hall inspecting the building. I am admiring the way Paul and his friends have fixed the walls, and Paul is shouting down from the scaffolding, and his friend Rob is saying, 'Should be done in a couple of weeks.'

I am feeling pretty pleased with myself.

All my own, I am thinking. Mine and Paul's.

No Cassandra at all.

I have a treacherous yearning for independence, not that I haven't learned various life skills from my experience as Cassandra's colleague or assistant, but I now feel it might be time to branch out on my own.

I am thinking how very clever we have been.

Then I see a madman running up the hill towards me.

He's an angry little madman, and by the time I see him he's really hopping around and waving his arms. He's danced himself into a merry rage and he is apparently shouting, 'THE BATS, THE BATS,' though that seems such a blatantly ludicrous thing to be shouting up a hillside that at first I don't quite trust my senses.

Paul comes down from the scaffolding, with Rob behind him.

'What's he saying?' says Paul, as the man careers towards us, waving his arms.

'Something about bats, I think,' I say.

'Bats?' says Rob.

And we stand and stare. We stare at this wizened lunatic, who is explaining — dancing on the spot and screaming at the top of his lungs — that a population of special bats lives at Frith Hall. These bats have been there for years. As soon as the place was abandoned the bats moved in. They perform elegant sonar-assisted circles around the hall, and they are protected bats. They are protected by law.

The hopping lunatic adds that no mere humans can use Frith Hall because the bats are so very important.

The bats are so important that Frith Hall

has to stay empty and ruined for eternity, so the bats can shit liberally across its walls and engage in boisterous bat frolics above the fireplace.

'Bats?' Paul says, still bemused, when the man has finished.

Yes, bats. Big bats. Special bats . . . Extraordinary bats with super powers . . .

'I hardly think Frith Hall was built to house bats, was it?' I say. 'I mean, I had a notion that it was originally built to house humans, strange as that may sound.'

'It is the bats' home,' says the man. 'If you continue with what you're doing, you are casting them out of their home.'

I nearly laugh. I want to get the guy by the neck. Then I have an impulse to run down to White Farm for a blunderbuss and show him just what I think about his protected bats.

'Do you genuinely think that bats are more important than people?' I say.

He says, 'Live and let live. They can't defend themselves.'

'Who are you anyway?' I say.

'I'm Rodney Stipps. I live down at Setter Brow,' says the man. 'I work for the council.'

'Rodney. What would happen if we escorted all the bats — kindly, courteously — off the premises and took them to another suitable bat residence, of your choosing?' says Paul.

'I don't think that would be possible.'

Rodney is all puffed up and righteous, and he keeps looking over at his beloved clouds of bats, as if they are listening to his every word. As if they are cheering him on.

'They're just rats with wings,' says Paul.

'That's a terrible thing to say,' says Rodney with an apologetic glance at his followers.

'Well your objections have been noted,' I say.

'Do you understand what I am saying? I am saying that there is a prohibition on rebuilding because of the . . . '

'Yes, the bats,' we all say.

As Rodney bat saviour hops down the hill, I look back at the whirling torrents of bats and I think how ironic, that our plans for Frith Hall have been trashed by a cloud of flying gerbils.

Later I tell Cassandra and she barely even listens.

She says, 'Oh well, never mind.'

She has all her campaign charts on the table. Under the flickering light of a gas lamp she masses her armies.

Twenty people down at Duddon Beck. Thirty-four people up on Birker Fell. Twenty-one out at High Wray Farm.

Then a load in Wales and Cornwall and probably scattered bands around the country she hasn't told me about.

'But Rodney will tell his friends,' I say. 'All the bat lovers will come to defend their hallowed bat shrine.'

'Don't worry, we'll be OK,' she says.

'What will we do?'

'Something.'

'Aren't you going to tell me?'

'I haven't finished working out the plan yet.'

'But do you agree with the basic principle that you should keep me informed?'

She looks at me and says, 'You're the one who went off and caused a lot of fuss at Frith Hall without telling me.'

'I wanted it to be a nice surprise.'

'Well, then I have some surprises planned for you too.'

'Nice surprises?'

'Of course.'

When Cassandra is calm like this she scares me the most.

'How many people know what's really going on?' I say.

'Quite a few around here. Then some others beyond. But I'm quite happy to claim they didn't, if it comes to that. Still' — and she pauses thoughtfully — 'I'm afraid the tripwires in their gardens might contradict my testimony.'

'But the Yateses? The Williamses? The Wadsworths? The rest of the ancient and infirm? Do they know?'

'No, they haven't a clue.'

'Are you going to tell them?'

'Of course not,' she says. 'It would only upset them.'

When her gang comes in for tea she says to them, 'All along these people have shafted us. The council has shafted us. They set up all these restrictions on building. They protect half the buildings and no one can convert a barn so someone can live in it. Then they sell the remaining few properties to the highest bidder. No allowances for locals. No schemes to keep permanent residents in the area. No, they just flog off whatever they have to the highest bidders, the greedy freaks. And then the owners have shafted us. Oh they've been so very courteous, but they've shafted us anyway. They come once every five years and they smile away at us, as if we should be friendly to them. They give us a patronising wave and sometimes, oh, if we're really lucky, they dine in our shitty little pubs or cafés, though they feel they are slumming it rather, but they're oh so sporting and they tuck into their steak and kidney pies with a saintly air, and they say, 'Mmm, very good,' when we clear the plates away. And what they mean is, 'Very good considering . . . Considering you are the rustic poor, and know very little of refinement.' Then they drive off again in their big shining cars and that's it for another half-decade or so. They never enquire into our lives and so they never understand how grave their offence is.

'Who are the building restrictions for? The perverts. No one else benefits from them.

'And we've sat back for years, and simply accepted it. And now — are you prepared to fight? Are YOU?'

She stares at each one in turn. Some of them are young, and others look more time-addled, but they all seem genuinely steadfast. Not one of them doubts her at all.

★ ★ ★

'But what are you going to do?' I say, again. 'Just what is the plan?'

She says, 'You'll find out soon enough.'

23

There is a notice.

Signed by the council, or the bat worshipper, or someone who simply loves bats. Stuck to the side of Frith Hall.

We just can't get enough bat, says the notice. We love bat. UP with bats. Bats forever. And then it says:

Redevelopment of this land contravenes article 2.34 of the Protected Species Act and will lead to prosecution in a court of law.

Then there's a violent rainstorm, and so the next day the notice says:

Re . . . lop . . . his . . . and . . . ven . . . 2.3 . . .
Pro . . . Spec . . . nd . . . ll . . . ad . . . pro . . .
t . . . a . . . c . . . ut . . . law

'Well, that's a shame,' says Paul.

We stand in silence while the wind blasts through the ruin and tugs at our clothes. The bats have won. Perhaps they are even gloating in their inaudible way; they seem to have a jaunty look about them as they hang upside down and squeak at each other.

'There is one thing we can do,' says Paul.

I say, 'Really? Do tell.'

He is shrugging because as we both know precisely what he means there is little point in indulging in further discussion, and then we go into the bat palace and undress each other among the abandoned scaffolding and the reek of bats.

I offer up a prayer to thee, O bats, that I may not have desecrated this thy sanctuary, that I may not have disturbed thee by the violence of my moaning or my excessive invocations of Jesus and the Virgin Mary.

I pray that thou shalt all settle down again to thy fulfilling existence in this lonely ruin, undisturbed by builders or the further sound of anyone saying FUCK.

And Paul says Jesus Christ FUCK and I say Mother of God FUCK, and then we drag on our clothes, suddenly aware of the cold again.

★ ★ ★

When I go back to the farm there's a Frenchman standing in the living room, looking slightly fazed. He tells me he's called François. I tell him that's great, and we are standing in silence when Cassandra comes in and says, 'Bonsoir, François. Comment ça va?'

François, it turns out, is our agent in France.

I just nod. 'OK,' I say, when Cassandra explains.

Events have long since slipped out of my grasp.

It seems I am just along for the ride.

Or I am running to catch the bus, which is speeding away from me, with Cassandra at the wheel.

I am running to catch the bus, even though Cassandra is driving full speed towards a great gaping precipice.

For some reason I want to be on the bus anyway, though the chasm is opening up before us and there's simply no way Cassandra can turn the bus around . . .

Anyway, she doesn't want to turn it.

She wants to hurl it straight into the abyss.

★ ★ ★

'And is it true that there's a resettlement scheme in Tuscany?' says Mandy at Wolf Barn.

'I don't know,' I say. 'I don't know anything.'

Later Mandy stops asking questions, because by then she's decided to leave.

Later she just says in her devout way that she is very disappointed that we lied to her, and besides what did we think we were doing?

She gathers her bags and her children and her foul-smelling boyfriend Peter and she marches down the drive.

Shaking her head.

'What a waste of my time,' she says, Peter sauntering alongside her. Initially he didn't seem to care too much, but once Mandy had started on her sermon he had to back her up.

It turns out Paul is to blame for the information leak.

Paul decided the time had come that everyone at Wolf Barn knew the truth. It had gone too far, he decided. They should decide whether to stay or to go on the basis of real knowledge.

I understood what he meant because I was getting pretty tired of Cassandra changing the plot all the time without letting me know. Equally, Paul didn't have the faintest idea what was actually going on, but he told the others what he knew and after that there was a big stunned silence and then they started shouting.

Mandy packed up first because she didn't want her kids to be involved. Some others did the same. They took their bags and their pot plants and their kids and their dogs and arranged for lifts to Foxfield station.

As she was leaving, Mandy said, 'Why did you have to spoil everything, Paul?'

Mandy didn't want the truth at all.

She wanted her Cassandra White as a druid version.

Her Cassandra White on her big white horse version.

Her Cassandra White runs naked in the moonlight while fairies plait her tresses version.

Mandy shook her head reproachfully at Paul and he said he was sorry, and then she left.

Anyway that sorted out the chaff.

All the undecided and barely committed went marching off down the valley, and the remaining occupants of Wolf Barn started building a tall fence and setting a series of traps and alarms. They made a bell that jangled if the gate was moved. It was as raucous as a fire alarm and there was no way anyone could miss it.

Then they made a set of tripwires and a big

pit covered with leaves. They put bales of straw at the bottom, to break the intruder's fall.

That was the ingenious invention of a man called Mickey, an ancient grizzled bloke who looked as if he had set a few traps before.

'National Service,' he said, and everyone just nodded and left him to it.

Now any intruder — or rather the actual legal owner of the house — would have to get through a series of obstructions including:

The locked and bolted gate, preventing any vehicle from being driven through.

The alarm bell triggered by anyone trying to force the gate.

The first set of tripwires.

The pit.

The sand swamp.

The enormous bolted gates in front of the main complex.

The electric fence.

The second set of tripwires.

The moat — a wide channel of diverted river.

And then the locks and bolts on the houses.

And the armed and ready occupants.

★ ★ ★

'Do you think you did the right thing, Paul?' I say.

'Yes,' he says.

'No sense of lurking doubt or unease?'

'No.'

Cassandra has a theory, I tell him, that if you defy the law enough then it starts supporting you. If you take a listed building and trash it utterly with some piece of entirely inappropriate interior design, then it's only in the early years that anyone can get you. They can come and make things miserable for you, tell you to take it all down, put back the nice old wall you battered down to make way for your open-plan living room and generally erase all traces of your presence from the venerable building. But if your interior design horror abides for years, then no one can do anything. Persistence is the key, she always says. If you're going to do something bad, then do it for a long time and eventually you transcend the law.

You just can't be half-hearted. If you refuse to pay any tax at all and take yourself away to a tax haven, no one does anything at all. It's only if you're diffident about it, if you just stop at filling in a slightly dodgy tax return. Then you're smashed into a pulp and flayed by the sentinels. If you have the wealth to be decisive, to waltz off and buy another house in Switzerland, they don't do anything at all.

If you are excessive enough then you pass into a realm beyond the law.

If you are going to be a tyrant and an adulterer and a fraudster, then make sure you are the president.

If you are going to squat in other people's houses, then make sure you squat in thousands of them.

Make sure you take over five valleys and somewhere in Wales. And a Cornish fishing village. And some undisclosed region of France.

When I have finished, Paul smiles at me and puts his hand on mine.

'People keep telling me what Cassandra thinks about everything. But what about you? What do you think about it all?'

'No one ever asks me.'

'I'm asking you.'

And I don't know what to say.

★　★　★

Beckfoot is fortified. There is a fence around the place, and a padlock on the gate. Locks on all the windows, all the ones Banker Sooke hadn't locked up already.

Well, he was right to be afraid.

★　★　★

Cassandra stalks around the yard, giving orders.

Vegetables are gathered. Pigs are mucked out. Wood is brought in.

It's a clockwork process, White Farm. Precision planned. Food is distributed among the resettlers. Supplies come in from Wolf Barn. Supplies go out to other resettlers. Grateful resettlers bring their offerings. Vegetables are gathered.

★　★　★

Wilton Mill is just about fortified. Riverbank is just about fortified. The valley is just about fortified, shambolic bits of netting and the baroque workings of Mickey and a few deep dark holes in the ground. Then there are Mrs Morgan and Mr Willis, watching out of their windows. If the perverts come when they've just popped into Barrow, or gone to buy buns in Broughton-in-Furness, then I don't know what we'll do.

'You're always finding something to worry about,' says Cassandra. 'It'll be fine. They never go out. Mrs Morgan hasn't left the house for about twenty-two years.'

The farmer goes past on his tractor and salutes me. I salute him back.

24

In the dead of night, Banker Sooke returns.

He's determined to sneak up on us. He is wily and secretive and neglects to employ our informant cleaner. He arrives long after Mrs Morgan and Mr Willis have gone to sleep. He conspicuously fails to announce his return. He drives along the valley in his sleek black BMW, under the cover of darkness. He doesn't suspect a thing.

With touching naivety he expects to find his house silent and empty. The whirlpool unsullied and the beds unused. He expects to find only the rich perfume of antique mahogany and nothing else, nothing like rose water and strawberries and PG Tips, and he assumes the garden will be as meaninglessly landscaped as ever before.

Steeped in his inaccurate version of reality Banker Sooke suspects nothing until he parks his car by the gate and sees there is a light on in his house — the innocent old Williamses sitting in his living room, watching *Newsnight*. The Yateses are in bed in the Chinese room, having turned in early after a hard day tending the garden and drinking tea.

And Banker Sooke stands by his car thinking — I expect — 'How strange. Strange indeed, but how did the lights get switched on?' Because he's been so very unforthcoming about his plans he can hardly complain when he walks up to the gate and finds it locked against him. Had he given us any warning we would have made all the necessary arrangements.

Even a day, even an hour, and we would have cleared out the Yateses and the Williamses and scoured the place for stray curlers.

We would have whipped the packets of cake mix out of the larder and wiped tea off the upholstery.

We would have puffed up all the puffs and thrown all the throws.

But because Banker Sooke has been so determinedly mysterious the gate is slammed shut and though he jangles the bars he can't move it. He thinks perhaps, did I forget to oil it? Has it frozen up? He jangles it some more and then he finds a big heavy padlock. His gate is locked against him. This causes him a few basic problems of understanding. Though his clever mind is racing through probabilities and plausible solutions, Banker Sooke is frankly confused. He can assess an interest rate in a second, but faced with the violent unlikelihood of a padlock on his gate Sooke's brain stalls. There's a moment when, perhaps, he thinks he has come to the wrong house. Is this really mine? he thinks, and then he remembers it really is.

It is then that Banker Sooke begins to lose his temper. He hammers on the gate again. He makes an initially decent attempt at climbing over it, but then he slips in the darkness and nearly brains himself on the spikes. This makes him so furious that the Williamses are quite afraid. We hear their trembling voices down the phone, as Cassandra says, 'There's actually a madman outside your house?'

'He seems to be very angry indeed,' Mavis is saying. 'He's shouting about how we're trespassing on his property and he's going to kill us.'

And she lets out a short scream.

⋆ ⋆ ⋆

Cassandra looks around the room. I am there, bleary eyed but swiftly becoming alert, pulling on my boots, and there are ten others awaiting instructions. I am thinking about Banker Sooke and just how bewildering it must all seem to him. For a brief second I even feel a mild spasm of pity for him, finding his house converted into a pensioners' lodge.

A very mild spasm, which passes instantly.

'Mavis, don't do anything,' says Cassandra. 'Stay inside, don't communicate in any way with the madman, and we will be there in a moment.'

★ ★ ★

With Beckfoot it began and with Beckfoot it will end, I think, as I run along with the pack, up the hill. Cassandra is already far ahead, bounding up the rocks, her body rigid with determination. There's some light from a pasty gibbous moon, but it keeps vanishing behind the clouds. When the moon disappears I stumble on the snowy ground, trying not to fall.

We pass the yew tree and the burial ground and I'm remembering the day Cassandra and I first found Beckfoot and how really I should have been firmer with her from the start. But it's easy enough to think like that when you are running in the cold night air with your weary body protesting all the way and the spectre of an enraged banker before you.

It is easy to think all sorts of things like what have I done and who has been driving me to act all these months, a force within or the personality of Cassandra, and do I have any autonomy or individual agency and who am I anyway and what is this reality around me and it's easy to become a hunch-backed existentialist, in the night, with the sounds of a scuffle developing ahead of you.

I run on nonetheless because aside from my rising fear there's a base desire, a curious insistent urge to see the banker himself. So I go through the gate — now dragged open — and see Cassandra and a couple of others forcing a man into the shed. This is Sooke, surprisingly enough, and he is tall and fairly fat, and his face is obscured by Cassandra's arm, but it's clear he is resisting and in a shrill frightened voice he is shouting, 'YOU BASTARDS, WHO ARE YOU BASTARDS? WHAT THE FUCK ARE YOU DOING?'

Like a condemned man, struggling against the noose, Banker Sooke is trembling and crying, 'LET ME GO! LET ME GO! You freaks! You bastard shits!'

Despite all that, they push him into the shed and Cassandra slams the door as he scrabbles to push it open and with a brief triumphant smile she turns the key.

Inside his shed Banker Sooke carries on shouting, 'LET ME OUT LET ME OUT WHAT THE HELL IS GOING ON I DEMAND YOU LET ME OUT . . . '

Now his screams are muffled because he's in a woodshed in a garden — his woodshed, his garden, lest we seem ungrateful — though it's clear enough what he's trying to express. It's clear that Banker Sooke is very angry indeed. And very afraid.

★　★　★

When I go inside I find Mavis lying on the sofa, looking faint, while Arthur fumbles in the kitchen, trying to make her a cup of tea.

'I'll do that,' I say because he keeps dropping the bags and waving the kettle around as if he's intent on sustaining third degree burns.

Cassandra is sitting next to Mavis, looking quite the concerned and upright widow. Her gang has tactfully dispersed.

'Oh it was dreadful,' Mavis is moaning. 'I thought he was going to kill us both.'

'Don't worry,' says Cassandra, patting her hand. 'It'll all be fine.'

'But there's a psychopath in the woodshed,' says Mavis, in a tearful voice.

'He won't be there long,' says Cassandra.

'When will the police get here?' says Arthur, and of course, 'Never, I hope,' is the answer that springs immediately to mind, and Cassandra says, 'Don't worry. Everything is being taken care of. You go to bed now.'

'But won't they need us to give a statement?' says Arthur.

'I'll wake you when you're needed,' says Cassandra.

'I don't think I'll ever sleep again,' says Mavis.

The Yateses have slept through everything, which we all think is great good fortune at the time, but which turns out to be a mighty disaster.

'Now it's quiet, I don't think we should disturb them,' says Cassandra.

She says that firmly, in the tone of the decent upstanding citizen she so entirely isn't, and everyone nods as if she is quite right.

Then we go into the night thinking we have at least postponed the catastrophe, and when we get back to White Farm Cassandra says, 'We may as well keep Banker Sooke imprisoned for a few days. Work out what to do with him.'

And I say, 'Shouldn't we move him somewhere else? I don't think we can keep him there very long.'

'We'll move him over here tomorrow morning. Get some sleep.'

* * *

240

With Beckfoot we began and with Beckfoot we fell, in one of those pristine pieces of irony that you admire even as you succumb to it.

Even as we tumbled into disarray and violence, I couldn't help but acknowledge the perfection of that irony, as if we were after all the powerless pawns of some deus ex machina that still insisted on punishing hubris.

If anyone was going to get punished for hubris, we were perfectly suitable candidates, having blithely ignored sundry laws and really been cavalierly indifferent to the prevailing mores of our society. As well as relatively contemptuous of notions of an omniscient deity and so forth.

All of that was bad enough, and then Cassandra made the peculiar decision to leave the Yateses asleep.

Thereby we failed to tell them what had happened, or what we were claiming had happened.

We failed to explain that if they heard a crazed maniac shrieking from the shed then they weren't to worry.

They weren't to do anything and, particularly and most importantly, they weren't to go up to the shed and start asking the maniac if there was anything troubling him and how they could help him.

Thereby we failed to prepare Tabitha Yates for the surprising noises she heard when she wandered from her bed at three a.m. and went downstairs to make a cup of tea.

★ ★ ★

The first I know about the trouble we're in is when I'm woken again by noises below. I'm lying in my cold bed, and there's not a hint of light around the curtains. It's long before dawn, and yet I'm hearing some shouting and the general noise of frantic activity. Thuds and crashes, urgent footfalls up- and downstairs.

Then it sounds as if Cassandra is roaring, 'The POLICE, the POLICE.'

The police, I think.

In my confusion I think, well, what's the big fuss about the police?

Why are we worried about the police?

Aren't the police generally to be welcomed, a reassuring presence, just the sort of people you want to see?

I am halfway downstairs and preparing to tell Cassandra to stop shouting about nothing and then suddenly I ascend into alertness and think, FUCK, the POLICE.

'Who the fuck called the police?' I roar myself, as I arrive in the study to find

Cassandra on the phone, ringing anyone she can think of.

'I don't know,' she says. 'But they've passed the checkpoint and they're coming along the road.'

That means we've fifteen minutes and then the police will be upon us.

Fifteen minutes, I think. Not so much time after all.

I could call my mother and explain that she might not be hearing from me for a while. I could explain to Cassandra that it's been wonderful working with her, and that I will always admire her, but it turns out I really have to go. I could find Paul Bowness and say goodbye.

I could do one of these things but not all of them.

And my helpful inner voice — so ignored of late, so entirely squashed — is saying: *Go now. Go while you can. Gather your things, or don't even gather them. Just GO.*

Ever since I arrived here, ever since the first day, that steadfast voice has been telling me to leave.

It has been exhorting me regularly to get the hell out of White Farm.

And I have ignored it every time.

I have denied its every urging and now I am standing at the doorway watching

Cassandra, who is coming from the wood-shed holding a blunderbuss. In the night a storm has blown up, so she is running into the wind, her head bowed. I'm shouting, 'What are you doing with that gun?' as she runs into the garden and fires three shots in the air.

'I'm going to bloody Beckfoot,' she shouts back at me.

'Then I'm coming,' I say.

'Do whatever you want,' she says, and then she charges off, holding her gun in the air.

★   ★   ★

The deus ex machina came to screw with us in the form of a creeping insomniacal old woman, Tabitha Yates, woken by her feeble bladder.

Tabitha Yates, unaware of the star part the deus had given her, oblivious to her sudden significance, went wandering downstairs in her nightgown to make a cup of tea.

Because she was unwitting, because we had kept her ignorant from the start and left her sleeping even when Sooke arrived, Tabitha heard a strange noise and couldn't think what it was.

As she waited for the kettle to boil, Tabitha heard a mighty banging in the garden and the sound — yes, gradually she identified it — the sound of screaming.

And being an old woman with a bizarre death wish, or certainly lacking any of the admirable caution the Williamses had shown, Tabitha Yates decided to get a torch and go out in her dressing gown to see what was happening.

The deus ex machina urging her along.

In her nylon dressing gown she walked down the garden path, the torch casting a faint circle of light on the grass.

Showing the trees in sullen monochrome.

And Tabitha was halfway down the garden path when she heard, 'LET ME OUT!'

'PLEASE LET ME GO. I HAVE MONEY. I CAN PAY YOU.'

Approaching the shed she heard the sound of sobs. An urgent desperate sobbing, and then the man was pleading, 'MY WIFE WILL BE WORRIED. I HAVE TWO YOUNG CHILDREN. I HAVE TO TELL THEM I'M ALL RIGHT.'

SOB, SNORT, SOB, said the banker.

'Who are you?' said Tabitha Yates, in her trembling old woman's voice, her flimsy dressing gown billowing in the wind. 'Why are you in the woodshed?'

'Who are you?' sobbed Banker Sooke.

'I'm Mrs Yates, I just heard you shouting

and came to see what the matter was.'

And at the sound of her kindly and even quavering tones, the tones of pure elderly decency, at the sound of someone who seemed unlikely to murder him, Banker Sooke began to cry harder, and in between his tearing sobs he said, 'Please open the door. Please let me out. I beg you.'

★ ★ ★

And now we come to the next error. For some reason Cassandra had decided to leave the key in the shed door. This was a piece of such startling carelessness that it makes me suspect she actually wanted the whole thing to unravel. There was always this not even latent urge to self-destruction in her, this lack of caution, bred of her feeling that she had already lost everything.

It attracted all those disciples, those devout followers who hung on her every word. They liked it because they thought it was courage, but really it was a total loss of inhibition, the normal preserving instinct that makes most of us hold off from really crazed behaviour. It was compelling, it drew you along.

It certainly drew me along, so perhaps all this means that I'm just trying to exonerate myself.

I suppose it's the sort of thing people say: 'I was a weak-headed imbecile and they had a certain inner strength.'

'They led and I followed.'

That isn't really it at all. I was hardly coerced. I wanted to be led. I wanted to be driven towards the precipice.

A sheep led by a demented sheepdog.

Ushered towards certain destruction.

★　★　★

Banker Sooke pleaded and Tabitha Yates stood there in her dressing gown, trembling with pity for the poor man, but somehow incurious as to why exactly he was in the woodshed and who had put him there.

★　★　★

'But why didn't you ask?'

'Well, he seemed so upset.'

'But why didn't you wonder how he had actually got into the woodshed?'

'I don't know. He was crying.'

'But why didn't you ask him who had put him there?'

'I just didn't think to . . . '

★　★　★

At this fate-burdened moment the key was in the shed door and all Tabitha Yates had to do was turn it.

And Banker Sooke was free.

Emerging from the shed, he saw an old woman with something like Parkinson's disease, trembling towards him, and she was saying, 'Would you like a cup of tea?' but Banker Sooke had recovered some of his former spirit and he said, 'No I fucking wouldn't. Get out of my way.'

And without a glance backwards, Banker Sooke was running towards the gate and this time unbridled fear made him scale it in an instant. And Tabitha was left with the key in her hand thinking, 'Well! Well! What a very rude man!'

Banker Sooke was free. Seething with rage. Trembling in his panic. And he raced back to his car — ah yes, finally someone had done something right, and remembered to take Banker Sooke's keys from his pocket. Yes, Cassandra actually had the keys to Banker Sooke's zippy BMW on her desk at home and Banker Sooke was left biting his hands with rage and desperation.

He did have his mobile phone, however, which was another major error on our part, and so he went running up the hillside — a hillside he had never thought to climb before

— to try to find some reception.

Because the Duddon Valley is one of only about three places in Britain where you still can't use a mobile phone.

Banker Sooke went running up the hill waving his phone in the air, wearing entirely impractical designer brogues, no good at all on the icy ground, and with nothing more than a thin jacket to protect him from the wind. He went sliding and shivering up the path and falling into hedges and scratching his polished skin on piles of gorse and rocks and all the time he was urgently banging his phone and shouting, 'Work, you piece of shit. WORK.'

★ ★ ★

There is great confusion at Beckfoot. Tabitha is twittering in the living room. She is twittering like a diseased sparrow. 'But he seemed so respectable, when he was in the shed. I would never have let him out had I not thought he was respectable. He just seemed very unhappy. He was worried about his wife and children. He kept begging me. He was crying. It was only when he came out that he was . . . oh . . . horrible . . . '

Oh, horrible indeed . . .

'You actually unlocked the door?' says Cassandra, in disbelief.

Tabitha is beginning to cry. 'He asked me to. He said please.'

The Williamses are white. Both of them, white as ice.

'What will we do?' Arthur says.

'Well, we must go and look for him,' says Cassandra.

And I am thinking, what kind of chaos is this? What sort of unholy madness have we settled into?

'Why haven't the police come?' says Arthur.

'Oh, they'll be here soon enough,' says Cassandra.

A plan, a sketchy knocked-about scheme, is unsteadily fashioned. Cassandra takes me into the garden — the shed door swinging jauntily in the wind — and tells me that the Williamses and Yateses must be taken back to White Farm. At least there they won't be trespassing. They must be told to stay there and not to talk to anyone. Some of the disciples will come and clear their stuff out of Beckfoot.

This is the plan.

It will not work and we both know it.

'The thing is in tatters,' I say.

'There's no need for that sort of talk,' says

Cassandra. 'Our greatest moment is about to come.'

'And our greatest moment is?'

'Victory through immolation,' she says triumphantly.

'Great slogan,' I say. 'Really persuasive.'

I assume at that point that her use of the word 'immolation' is purely metaphorical.

I am left with the poor pensioners, following them around the house, picking up things. Encouraging them in a gentle voice. Yes, Mavis, of course you can take your green handbag. Oh, and here are your glasses. And here are your cough sweets. And here's your vapour rub. Oh, and here's your travelling blanket.

'Why do we have to leave?' says Arthur.

'Because the psychopath might return. With some of his friends,' says Cassandra.

His friends being the police.

In our vibrant world of creative inversions, Cassandra has made our aged resettlers very afraid. The Yateses are in an age-slowed version of a hurry, flinging everything they can into a couple of bags, trembling and forgetting where they put their hats and then after they've done that for far too long I say, 'OK, it's time — we really have to go,' and I think how the whole thing is quite sad in the end, that we wanted to help the Yateses and instead we've just moved them from place to place and disturbed them out of their wits.

'Don't we have to get all the other pensioners out?' I say to Cassandra. I hiss it to her as we wait outside for Mavis, who has forgotten her tablets.

'No time. We'll just have to hope their innocence saves them from prosecution. As planned.'

'Okaaaay,' I say.

'I'm going to look for that shitty little banker,' says Cassandra. And off she goes, without another word, even though I shout after her, 'What do I do?'

'But what's really happening?' I shout, but already she is vanishing out of sight.

Over the hill and far away.

25

Wolf Barn is dead. The whole place is shut up and barred when I get there and I have to try to force the gate and set off the alarm to rouse them. Then I wonder if they'll shoot me by accident, but all that happens is George rushes out with an air rifle and says, 'Get your hands up or I'll blow your head off,' and I say, 'George, put that down.'

'How do you know my name?' says George, still waving his gun, from which I deduce that he's drunk. Or even more stupid than I thought.

Paul is running across the courtyard, in bare feet and boxers, hardly looking as if he's going to repel all assailants, but when he sees George waving a gun at me he knocks him down with a fist.

Like a marionette, George goes down.

'Are you OK?' says Paul, fumbling with the fifteen bolts and then grabbing me as soon as he's opened the gate. 'Did he hurt you?' He is leading me towards the house, minding out for the tripwires and the pit and the other property-enhancing features we have added to Wolf Barn.

'I'm fine,' I say.

'Why are you wandering around at this time of the morning?' he says.

So I explain about the police and how they will be arriving at any minute.

Then we are inside and Paul starts shouting to everyone, telling them to wake up because it's all over.

They come down murmuring and some of them have already started to panic.

They're actually shocked.

Even Mickey is looking perplexed and fearful.

Even George — rubbing his head, twitching and eyeing Paul with resentment — has realised just what a parlous state we're in.

'What should we do?' they say.

I assume they're talking to Paul but then I see they're all looking at me.

'Well, Cassandra has a plan,' I say. 'She wants everyone to defend their houses for as long as they can. But if you're afraid or you don't want to get caught and punished, then you should go now.'

This doesn't seem like much of a rallying speech.

It will not be taking a prominent place in the history of rhetoric.

It does not allude to any fighting on the

beaches and there is a conspicuous failure to refer to our happy band of brothers and sisters or our green and pleasant land.

It turns out it's not much of a crowd pleaser.

'What do you mean, just run away?' says a man called Nigel I've never much liked.

'Well, the point is, no one should feel coerced,' I say.

'But Cassandra White says we're fighting a battle,' says Nigel. 'She says we're fighting for a noble cause.'

'Well, of course we are,' I say. 'I'm just saying it's your own free choice what you do now.'

'What would Cassandra White tell us to do?' one of them says.

'I expect she would tell you not to be cowed and to fight until the end,' I say. 'Or something like that.'

And they mutter away, giving me disappointed glances.

As they go off to pack, or perhaps some of them really are going to stay and fight, I tell Paul that I have to go and find Cassandra.

He shrugs. 'OK, then I'm coming with you.'

'No no,' I say. 'You should stay here.'

'Why would I do that?'

'Because this is your house.'

'I don't care. I'm coming with you.'

'But if you don't stay here, they'll do something really stupid.'

Looking around at this angry horde I wonder if they are labouring under some sort of delusion that they might actually win. I assumed they would all be working on the basis of glorious defeat as their best option, but now some of them are piling off to the woodshed to look for weapons and Nigel is saying, 'Victory, Victory, Victory.'

I think Paul understands what I mean. He says, 'I'm walking you as far as the river anyway.'

Into the sullen storm we walk. The clouds are flying across the sky, chased by overbearing winds. The rain has stopped, but the wind keeps pushing us backwards. We stoop against it, heads bowed, through the forest and into the fields, the familiar track.

And my heart judders each time I see headlights on the road beyond the river.

'They must be up here by now,' says Paul.

'What will happen?' I say.

He grabs my arm. 'You have to make sure you're not caught. Please say you will?'

'What about you?'

'I'll be fine.' He smiles his jauntiest smile and kisses me.

Then we leap a foot from the earth,

because suddenly there's the sound — inescapable, unambiguous — of gunfire.

And there's an answering siren and then some tinny speech through a loudspeaker. I can't make out the words.

'My God,' I say.

'They must be shooting at Cassandra. Or she's shooting at them.'

'OK, I'm going over this river,' I say.

'Don't be an idiot.' He grabs my arm and starts dragging me away from the river.

That makes me angry so I throw him off. I push him away and I jump into the middle of the river. When I find my feet I'm in water up to my waist and it's running swiftly. I'm so cold that for a moment I think I have been encased in ice and they will find my fossilised remains in a million years time. Duddon woman, they'll call me. Apparent cause of death, an ill-advised dip in a winter river. It's cold beyond ordinary definable cold. My body is just stunned. So stunned it goes rigid, and for a while I can't move.

Paul wades in after me.

'What the hell are you doing? Are you trying to drown us both?'

'Well, it might be better than getting shot,' I say.

In the middle of the rushing river Paul explains, with surprising eloquence, given the circumstances, that he thinks drowning isn't actually preferable to getting shot and anyway it isn't strictly necessary to do one or the other, and why don't I come back to Wolf Barn with him, as it will be much safer to be there than racing around the fells when Cassandra has clearly gone wild with a blunderbuss and that before we discuss this further — pros and cons, waiting it out in Wolf Barn versus mad saunter up the fells — we should get out of the river.

I pretend to be going along with him. I say, 'Yes, OK, of course. You're perfectly right.' Together we wade back to the shore — the allegedly safe shore, where no one is shooting anyone yet. He holds me tightly and says, 'We have to get back, to get some dry clothes. Let's run for it — as fast as you can.' I kiss him hard, wanting to tell him something that he will remember later, but then I don't want to rouse his suspicions. So he assumes I am just recognising the prevailing logic of his argument and says, 'Come on, run fast, we have to go, now.'

He sets a fine pace, shouting back at me every so often, hurrying me along, offering words of encouragement, and at first I keep pace, I shout back, 'I'm right behind you,' but when he turns a corner ahead of me I spin round and start hurtling back towards the river. I don't know when he realises I've gone, because as soon as I get to the bank I rush into the water and swim across as fast as I can and then I'm out on the other side, racing through the heather, cold beyond belief and wondering if I will just die here and now. I think of him running along the path back to Wolf Barn and shouting back to me and then his sad sweet face when he realises I've gone. But I'm a fool and for some reason I have to find out how it ends. What crazy finale Cassandra is about to devise.

I shiver and curse and jog over the undulating fields until I reach the mud-caked lane to White Farm. Everything is quiet. I'm running through the garden, shouting, 'Cassandra! It's me! What's going on? Where are you? Don't shoot me with the bloody blunderbuss. Where are you?' I'm nearly at the house when I hear, 'Psst, in here . . . Psst . . . ' coming from the woodshed.

Inside there's a ratty looking girl called Madge. Cowering against an unheroic backdrop of mould and spiders.

'What are you doing in the woodshed?' I say.

'Regrouping.'

'Where are the Williamses and the Yateses?'

'The police took them.'

'Who the hell let that happen?'

Ratty Madge is looking pretty upset about it all.

'There was nothing we could do,' she says, with a wobbling lip. 'Old Mr Williams saw them coming and he ran down the drive and waved at them to stop. He was most indignant. 'You at last, where on earth have you been, I've been paying taxes all my life and the one night I'm besieged in my home up at Beckfoot by a psychopath you're nowhere to be seen. Had I not had the presence of mind to lock him in the woodshed there's no knowing what he would have done,' that sort of thing. Then the police said, 'You were up at Beckfoot?' and he said, 'Yes, that's where I live,' and they said, 'And you locked Mr Sooke in a woodshed?' and he said, 'I locked a dangerous madman in a shed, I don't care what he's called,' and Mr Williams was just getting on to how he lost five members of his family in the war and they had no right to ignore a pensioner like him when they pushed him into a police car and then they came and took his wife and the Yateses away.'

'What were you idiots doing all this time?'

'Most of the team had gone to set up roadblocks. Then the rest of us decided it was best if we avoided capture.'

'So you hid?'

'We avoided capture.'

'Why didn't you do something?'

'We decided there was no point in losing valuable people power.'

I roll my eyes at her.

'Well, you're doing a great job, in there in the shed. You're really helping.'

'I'm just waiting until the coast is clear.'

'Where are the other idiots?'

'The rest of the team is dispersed around the valley, at the various fighting stations,' she says.

She's trying to regain her dignity. But it's hard to muster any gravitas when you're squatting on a pile of damp wood and your hair is full of leaves.

'Where is Cassandra?'

'I'm afraid I'm not at liberty to tell you,' she says.

'Don't be ridiculous. Where is she?'

'She left strict instructions that her whereabouts were to be protected.'

'But not from me.'

'She didn't make any exceptions.'

'Well don't you think it's a bit ridiculous that you, the brazen coward in the woodshed, know where she is and I don't?'

She looks sulky and clamps her mouth.

So I march off to the house and I get all the papers and folders and every scrap I can find in Cassandra's study and I dump them all in a pile in the garden and pour kerosene all over them.

I light a rag and hurl it on the pile and stand back as the whole thing goes up with a satisfying boom.

Then I grab a stray blunderbuss and go back into the woodshed, where Madge the rat is still hiding and then I say, 'Where the fuck is Cassandra?'

And she says, with a mournful little smile, 'I knew you'd do something like that.'

Cassandra came down from the mountain and peppered a few policemen with shot. Madge tells me she hit each of them fair and square in the arse and sent them limping off, crying in rage. Then she headed up into the woods again. So the police — the ones who hadn't been taken away to have shot extracted from their rumps — drove a fleet of cars up to the edge of the wood and started saying things into their loudspeakers.

'COME OUT WITH YOUR HANDS UP.' 'COME OUT QUIETLY.' 'DROP YOUR GUN.' 'YOU DON'T HAVE TO DO THIS, MRS WHITE.'

Madge is just telling me this when all the alarms go off.

'Oh my God,' says Madge. 'What do we do now?'

I still have my blunderbuss trained on her.

'I'm only eighteen,' she says. 'I don't want to rot in jail.'

'OK.' I open the door for her and chuck the blunderbuss away. 'Go. There's no point defending this place. It does actually belong to Cassandra.'

And we both start running, out of the back door and through the orchard, and then we're tumbling into the woods.

Madge rat girl vanishes into the night. I suppose she doesn't really want to hang around with me any more. Anyway, she's squeaking with fright and she's clearly going to get caught before she's scuttled a dozen paces.

★ ★ ★

I can hear the thud of helicopter blades and every so often the ugly blare of a siren. Then they're chattering through their loudspeakers, trying to draw the fugitive out.

They've probably got some crack squad clambering up the mountain, to get a better view of the woods.

I'm irresolute until it occurs to me that I know exactly where Cassandra is. I stand in the lower wood and pause for a moment, working out how I can get there without being caught. There are dogs barking near

Beckfoot, so I start running towards the river.

I hear another flash of sirens, and the sound of shots ricocheting around the hills.

In my panic I can barely remember the path. There's a broken fence without a stile. I struggle over it, barbed wire dragging at my clothes. Then I'm sliding across wet rocks, trying to keep my head down. There's a waterlogged field, where the mud encases my legs. That slows me down and makes me sick with nerves. When I get through I pause to vomit, and then I start running again, my boots now clogged with mud.

Down here, the sirens are faint, and then there's just the whirr of the helicopter and the distant chatter from the loudspeakers. I slide in the mud again, and then I'm dragging myself over another fence. I'm cursing vaguely, until I see the gorge ahead. Here the river churns into a tight channel, and suddenly the rocks rise on either side of it. I remember there's a sharp drop to my left — just in time, because the path vanishes and I almost fall over the carcass of a sheep. That was an unlucky sheep, I think as I go past it.

Now there's a line of trees to hide in. I don't think the police have got this far. It's a long way from the road and I've just been stopped by a deep bog and nearly tumbled into a ravine. I pick up pace as the ground becomes less sodden. There are sheep milling around, and I try not to set them scampering along. I stumble over uneven ground, stepping over roots and grabbing at branches. Really striving, straining with the effort, to not get caught.

I'm just reaching the line of yew trees when there's a hand on my shoulder and I just nearly die with fright.

'Sshh, don't say anything, come with me,' says Cassandra.

'What the fuck are you doing sneaking up on me?' I say.

'Sssh, we haven't time.'

And she drags me to the mountain track and we start climbing again.

26

Well, this is just about where we began.

Cassandra racing up the hill in a bitter storm and me offering vague and superfluous protests, imprecations, general observations on the futility of our actions and the disastrous nature of our predicament.

Then the surprise vision beneath us. The flames.

You can understand that I wasn't expecting the flames.

Cassandra had occasionally alluded to her great plan B but naturally she had never told me what plan B was. So we were standing on the hillside and Cassandra was waving her gun around, and all beneath us the valley was on fire.

Dozens of houses, florid with flame and Cassandra with her eyes glinting and full of reflected light, and saying, 'That must be the most beautiful thing I've ever seen.'

And the police cars blasting their sirens, and no one taking any notice.

'All the cowards have fled,' says Cassandra. 'Only the steadfast remain.'

Then she says, 'Come on, take this gun.'

'I don't want a gun.'

'You'll need it. Look what happened to the Williamses.'

She tosses a gun down behind her, and it clatters on the rocks.

'This is completely insane,' I say, but she's not listening. My words are whipped away by the wind.

I pick up the gun and keep climbing after her.

'What are you doing now?'

'Beckfoot must burn,' she's shouting back. 'Beckfoot must fucking burn.'

There's a helicopter above us, but it's flying towards the fires. It's buzzing like a moth to a flame, and Cassandra's above me, saying, 'Come on, I'll let you strike the first match.'

Beckfoot must burn.

I stand there on the rocks, catching my breath.

Beneath me, the Old Vicarage is burning. Riverbank is burning. Wilton Mill is burning.

Beckfoot must burn, Cassandra is shouting.

And I'm feeling pretty furious, in amongst my teeming confusion, because I'm beginning to realise that everyone else knew. Dozens of people must have known about Plan B, and yet Cassandra never told me.

Everything must burn.

Plan B was to torch the place.

And far from experiencing the thrill of accomplishing one's schemes, of an immaculate plan brought to glorious fruition, I am mostly feeling a deep sense of pique. I am struggling to understand why Cassandra neglected to tell me what she told everyone else.

Three shots in the air, and torch everything.

Three shots in the air, and take the petrol from the special cache, and light the matches, and leave the place to burn.

As planned.

I think of all those planning meetings I was never invited to attend.

All the discussions I never had.

Everything I failed to understand.

Three shots in the air, the coded signal, and now all of you to work.

All of you who know what's actually going on.

Meanwhile I was just hopping around the countryside, packed off to do something pointless. Sent off to fix a drain or build a wall or take tea to the old or goats to the young. I bridled at being called Cassandra's assistant but I wasn't even that. I was her janitor.

The helicopter is buzzing above the Old Vicarage, and now I see something that really makes me sick.

Wolf Barn is burning. There's a fire in the forest. The flames are rising above the trees, lighting all the forest as they climb.

And I think, et tu Bowness? Even you?

Cassandra has vanished behind a layer of rock, and now I am racing to catch up with her, I am panting and cursing and just as I reach Beckfoot — noting that Banker Sooke's BMW is still sitting there — I see Cassandra with her arm aloft and in her hand is a bottle.

A bottle. A Molotov cocktail, more like.

And as I am shouting, 'Are you sure this isn't going a bit far?' she hurls the bottle through the front door of the house, and the place explodes.

A violent burst of energy and ignition and then the brisk businesslike crackling of flames.

Here, too, Cassandra has been busy preparing her plan B.

Here, too, she has kept her real intentions entirely hidden.

Here, too, I am presented clearly with a sense of just how peripheral I have been to everything that was really important.

The final aim of this whole resettlement scheme.

The final aim was mighty destruction.

Fire and ash.

There is red fire behind the windows and then the sound of glass shattering. Cassandra is firing shots in the air. She is on the hillside above Beckfoot and I imagine her screaming, 'BURN EVERYTHING,' to the sheep and the rocks.

Poor Banker Sooke, I think. The wooden extension is going to look awfully wrecked tomorrow.

And all that beautifully tempered oak.

And oh what will become of the whirlpool?

What will become of the Regency period mahogany cane armchairs, with lotus-carved tapering front legs?

And the sofa table with lion's paw castors.

And the Chippendale-period gilt-wood mirror.

And the matching pair of celestial and terrestrial globes by G. and J. Cary of St James's Street London.

And the wine cellar.

This is no way to treat a Chateau Filhot 1937.

Now the helicopter is turning towards Beckfoot, buzzing up the valley and that makes me move quickly. The police cars are burning up the lane, sirens flashing. I hear more shots, Cassandra firing off her gun, or perhaps she's already found some other targets in the woods. I wonder how high she's got — if she's up at the sheepfold, or maybe even near the tarn.

I jump down from the rock and I start scrambling along, and with the buzzing loud in my ears I don't stop running until I've fallen into a sheepfold. Then I crouch by a wall and I see the flames rising and the helicopter shining a light on a figure running out of the woods.

Victory through immolation.

Cassandra is running. I can see her, a scrawny figure with a gun.

Racing across the fell.

And behind me I can hear:

'FOLLOW THAT WOMAN.' Through the loudspeakers, a tinny voice, 'FOLLOW THE CRAZY WIDOW.'

Follow the druid . . . follow the fairy queen . . .

A fairy queen with flaming hair and a gun full of shot.

I sneak uphill through the bracken, rustling in a furtive way. I'm hardly the star attraction but someone might just want to arrest me. For the sake of it, they might

271

just throw me in a cell. For want of anything else to do with me.

I hurtle along a sheep track and when I stop to catch my breath I can see Wolf Barn blazing like a furnace in the forest. And now as I grub along in the bracken, I hear a new noise, the rise and fall of a dozen fire engines, tearing over the hill from Barrow.

Screaming into the valley.

I'm nearly at the top of the fell, up on a stretch of weather-beaten grass and rock, and ahead I see it. The improbable sight. Cassandra crouched behind a rock, aiming her gun.

This time I sneak up on her. This time I rustle through the undergrowth towards her and I think she hasn't noticed me, but when I'm a metre away she says quietly, 'Why do you keep following me?'

'Why didn't you tell me about the fires? Why didn't you tell me the plan?'

'Sssh, get down, unless you want to get us killed.'

I bend down behind the rock and when I peer over briefly I can see what she's aiming at — a horde of approaching policemen, all of them moving swiftly, perhaps even nervously, through the bracken, silhouetted against the smoke and flames.

'Now you should go,' says Cassandra, waving her hand at me.

'What if I don't want to go?'

'Just go. Save yourself. Really, there's nothing else left to do now.'

Naturally I should just take the cue and go. There's that whole other side of the brain, neglected and cast out, saying, 'Just GO, you FOOL' and then there's my stubborn little ego, still confused and wanting to under-stand —

'But why didn't you invite me to the meetings? Why wasn't I there?'

'I didn't want you to come.'

'Why not?'

'I didn't want you to go to jail. There's nothing to link you to any of it. Anyone asks, you say you didn't know.'

'But what about the others? The ones who did know?'

'They'll be fine. They've got their orders. I wanted you to be able to go free. So you could just go back home, like it never happened, if you wanted to.'

'I don't want to.'

'Well, you might want to later,' says Cassandra briskly. 'So stop complaining.'

We are crouched side by side behind a rock. I look across at Cassandra, she looks across at me. I can't quite see the expression on her face.

'What happens now?' I say.

'You run as fast as you can across the valley.'

'And what do you do?'

'Oh, I have a few plans of my own.'

'What sort of plans?'

'You'll see,' she says, like she always does.

The policemen are getting closer, and I really think I shouldn't hang around, I think that I still could crawl backwards and I might even get away, even now. And all the time the police are saying through their loudhailers,

'That's all right, no need to do anything rash. Let's just come out quietly now . . . Let's be reasonable.'

And perhaps it's something in their encouraging tone, or perhaps I'm just in shock and while I'm trying to work out what the hell it is something quietly cracks. Or I crack, perhaps. I crack and in my cracked state I seize a gun.

And I say, 'I've had enough of this fucking nonsense.'

Even as Cassandra says, 'Get down,' I am getting up.

Then like a crazy cracked fool I run towards the police, yelling something, I can't quite remember what it was.

Something like 'NEAAAAARRRRRRRG'.

I am shouting and waving the gun in the air, and thinking that this can hardly be defined as reasonable.

Then I am shot.

27

The impact throws me to the ground.

I don't feel any real pain, just a sense of heat in my belly. I'm not quite sure what has happened at first, so I lie there very still and someone comes over to me, someone who isn't Cassandra, and there's a sound of static.

CRREUUUUUUUUK. CREEEEEEEEUKKK. Unit 2. Unit 2. We have a casualty. We have a casualty. CREEEEEEEEUUUUK.

Creeeeeeeeuk, goes the bracken and creeeueeek go the sheep, and creeeeeeeeuk go the birds above me.

And I suppose the storm is still raging because the clouds above are black and I think I feel rain on my face.

What a fine storm, I think, and then my head spins and I think I'm dying.

I must be dying because I see something which I suspect is a vision, I gain fleeting access to a parallel reality, somewhere quite beyond our chastened mortal realm, some-where even quite luminous.

I see a great green light and Cassandra is hovering beside me, or I guess we are both hovering somewhere, because I can't see the ground. No bracken or rocks or grass at all.

Cassandra tells me that all will be well, and that I must return to the planet — it seems we are not actually on the planet, 'This is a representation of a reality you understand, but fixed in no time at all,' Cassandra explains helpfully — and continue with our work.

And she says that although it may seem that life is harsh and bloody and the perverts always seem to win in the end, in fact there is great virtue and peace on the planet and this constantly counters the forces of perversion and destruction. So really you just have to hang in there and perhaps just perhaps you might be OK.

It's something like that anyway.

Then she waves her arm, and I see a great vista of verdant beauty, all the valley filled with sunshine and the fires have gone, and there are some lambs bleating and there's the sound of tractors thudding down the valley and birds gliding and casting their slender shadows on the hills. And Cassandra turns into a tree or I turn into a tree, or we both become trees and I think well who wants to be a tree, and I'm trying to say, no no, this has gone too far, please can someone help me to stop being a tree because however uplifting it is to see the sun shining across the fells who wants to be a tree?

And my arms are branches and I can't move them — I can't cry out —

I suppose I lose consciousness. Or regain it. I don't really know.

⋆ ⋆ ⋆

Events since then have been cloudy and indeterminate.

On the plus side, I recovered. The bullet had gone into my belly. My belly was altogether shot up and I had to spend some time in hospital. It was touch and go for a while, something about my mangled spleen, but I pulled through.

I lay there for weeks staring into space. I heard the police trying to talk to me and nurses saying I couldn't be disturbed and then I heard questions . . .

'But what did you think you were doing?'

'Can you tell us everything you remember?'

'We're certain you're an innocent victim in all of this, but can you help us?'

'We just want to make things as easy as possible for you.'

And I turned over and shut my eyes again.

I dreamed of fire and the smell of smoke. An acrid taste in my mouth. Carbonised rosewood, filling my lungs. I dreamed of pushing open the door of Beckfoot and finding Banker Sooke ablaze, and all his riches crumbled to ashes around him.

I dreamed of Cassandra with her green eyes, leaning over me, saying, 'Come on, really, time to get up.'

And the voices came again. 'Just speak slowly and tell us as much as you can.'

'We can sort something out for you.'

'We are here to find out what really happened to you.'

I pulled through, so really I should be thankful on that score. I should be delighted, not to be stark raving dead.

On the minus side I am now in a place that Cassandra wouldn't like at all. Cassandra would loathe it here but she's gone elsewhere or nowhere so it's simply impossible she would ever come to see me.

They told me she had filled White Farm with explosives. She had packed the place with dynamite, so after I got shot she ran down there. I suppose my crazy diversion gave her the chance to get home.

When they came to flush her out, when they massed at the farm gates and shouted through their loudspeakers, COME OUT MRS WHITE WITH YOUR HANDS UP, she just sent the place sky high.

I can't imagine what she was thinking as

the dynamite went off.

Hiisssssss

BOOOOOOM!

They found her by the duck pond.

Cassandra White died with her ducks.

The doctors tell me not to think about her and to keep myself busy with my work. So I sit in the office listening to the whir of the photocopier and the hum of dozens of computers and I try to focus on the flickering electronic lights which suck the moisture from your eyes.

They recovered me all the way to a little desk overlooking the car park, with a fine view of a rainbow spectrum of cars.

Green car. Blue car. Blue car drives away. Green car drives away. Blue car comes back. Red car. Green car comes back. Man gets out of green car. Red car comes back.

BOOOOOOM. Red car blasted into space. Flames chasing from one line of cars to the next. Metal twisting in the heat.

★　★　★

The valley was dark by the evening. They put out all the fires.

I don't really know what happened after that.

They told me I was very confused.

Apparently I had been eating a diet that only supplied me with 900 calories a day and someone argued that this had tampered with my faculties.

It turns out that quinoa does send you mad after all.

There was some concerned talk about diminished responsibility.

That seemed quite wrong to me. Then I was perfectly lucid. It's only now I have diminished responsibility.

My responsibility is well and truly diminished.

★   ★   ★

But I have my little chipboard desk and my view of the car park and I get an in-tray and an out-tray.

And I put things I have finished in the out-tray, like letters and invoices I have typed and then some gurning moron comes along and dumps a whole new pile of crap into my in-tray.

And I gurn back and say, 'Thanks very much.'

No one here knows what I really did.

The gun wound in my belly has cleared up now and there's just a little scorch mark where the bullet went in.

I eat about 4000 calories a day mostly in junk, and I drink enormous cups of coffee, which come out of a machine.

Straight from a big metal box into my styrofoam cup.

And I get my sandwich from the sandwich girl, white bread like flattened silicone with shiny tasteless tomatoes trapped inside. And they give me a Snickers bar for gurning so nicely.

★　★　★

They told me Paul Bowness didn't want to hear from me. Apparently that's something to do with his rehabilitation.

I have received no further visions.

I have not become a tree again.

No one here knows what I really did. They just think of me as the effortlessly tedious little freak who types the invoices. This is all part of my rehabilitation.

Apparently my error was to believe that I was anything other than a tedious little freak.

This is where I went so terribly wrong.

If I can only accept that tedious freakery is my preordained lot in life then I will be a happier and more popular person.

★　★　★

'Here you are, another invoice.'

'Well done freak, thanks so much.'

'Invoices for everyone!'

'Thank you, little freak. Have another five thousand memos to type.'

★　★　★

No one knows what I really did at all.

Anyway I'm meant to take a lot of pills to stop me caring about the boredom and the business of accepting my inner tedious freak, and all the other stuff in my head, but sometimes I forget to take them and that's when I start wondering. On the days when I am alert and quite unnumbed I think back to the time I spent in the valley and I think how someday maybe someday it will all happen again. I think to myself BOOOOOM just imagine if all this burned to smithereens if it all went BOOOOOM. And just imagine if the rich were usurped from their houses, if everything was turned upside down . . .

And on those days I stop typing, 'Dear Mr Bellow, We would like to offer you an altogether better deal on your life insurance' and instead I type

Everything will burn and the rich will find their houses burned

And the land will be ours

We will be free

The houses will burn the fat fucker houses with their mahogany tallboys and their rosewood serpentine desks and Mr Sooke will lie snivelling in his cell

And we will take back everything

And one day we will rise again.

★ ★ ★

That's what Cassandra told me.

We do hope that you have enjoyed reading this large print book.

Did you know that all of our titles are available for purchase?

We publish a wide range of high quality large print books including:
Romances, Mysteries, Classics
General Fiction
Non Fiction and Westerns

Special interest titles available in large print are:
The Little Oxford Dictionary
Music Book
Song Book
Hymn Book
Service Book

Also available from us courtesy of Oxford University Press:
Young Readers' Dictionary
(large print edition)
Young Readers' Thesaurus
(large print edition)

For further information or a free brochure, please contact us at:
Ulverscroft Large Print Books Ltd.,
The Green, Bradgate Road, Anstey,
Leicester, LE7 7FU, England.
Tel: (00 44) 0116 236 4325
Fax: (00 44) 0116 234 0205

A SMALL FORTUNE

Patricia Fawcett

When they win the lottery, Angela and Tom leave their roots and move to a designer home overlooking Morecambe Bay. Despite the money, Angela is discontented, and Tom changes — into a businessman with grandiose plans — whilst their daughter Melanie has no aim in life. A visit to Angela's sister, Moira, brings to a head their disparate relationships. Meanwhile, Tom's business plans unravel, bringing unexpected money worries, and Angela faces having to reveal that she's been sending money regularly to Cheryl, a woman who'd sent them a begging letter after the win. Should she trust her? Is Cheryl all she seems?